AFTERMATH

Look for other REMNANTS™
titles by K.A. Applegate:

Also by K.A. Applegate:
ANIMORPHS ®

REMNANTS ™

AFTERMATH

K.A. APPLEGATE

AN
APPLE
PAPERBACK

SCHOLASTIC INC.
New York Toronto London Auckland Sydney
Mexico City New Delhi Hong Kong Buenos Aires

ISBN 0-590-88522-7

Copyright © 2003 by Katherine Applegate.
All rights reserved. Published by Scholastic Inc.
SCHOLASTIC, APPLE PAPERBACKS, and associated logos are trademarks and/or registered trademarks of Scholastic Inc.
REMNANTS and associated logos are trademarks and/or registered trademarks of Katherine Applegate.

12 11 10 9 8 7 6 5 4 3 2 1   3 4 5 6 7 8/0

Printed in the U.S.A.   40
First printing, May 2003

For Michael and Jake

AFTERMATH

CHAPTER ONE

FIRST I GOT TO DEAL WITH SOME BEASTS.

Mo'Steel was a mess. His fingers and hands had been cut up by the sharp edges of his stolen Rider boomerang. His thigh boasted a gouge the size and color of a raw Mickey D's hamburger — except for where it oozed yellow-green pus. Antibiotics? Not happening.

Face it, 'migo, Mo'Steel thought. *If this infection doesn't clear up soon, you're toast.*

The slash across the front of his neck was maddeningly itchy, a good sign according to his mom, a sign that the wound was healing. She'd stitched his thigh as best she could, using thread made from plant fibers and an actual sewing needle from the days before the Rock, given — secretly — by a woman named Marina. She'd slipped the sewing stuff to Mo'Steel's mom with a warning against joining her son on such a dangerous journey with the Marauders. Olga had thanked Marina and gotten busy with her stitching.

Mo'Steel's neck had decided to close up on its own. Good.

Mo'Steel was no stranger to stitches, but in this very disturbing bizarro Earth, it was clear that those who were healthiest ruled. The fewer serious injuries, the better.

So, the Marauders couldn't know about the ache in his ribs where Hawk had sat on him, crushing his chest. Nor could they know about the pain caused by the popped shoulder joint, also courtesy of the big, bald, and seriously ugly Hawk.

Mo'Steel refused to let the Marauders know what real damage Hawk had done to him.

Hawk.

The Marauders' former leader. Mo'Steel's predecessor.

Man, this is so not good, Mo'Steel thought, not for the first time since waking up flat on his back in the Alpha bunker, surrounded by a ragtag group of Marauders, barely able to remember who he was, let alone how he'd gotten there.

And now the dream storm had finally passed and he was starting out on a journey through the Shadow Zone, into the Dark Zone, where a battle awaited him. A battle that would solidify his leadership or kill him.

Mo'Majesty. *Not yet,* he thought. *First I got to deal with some Beasts.*

"J'ou be careful," Echo said. She touched Jobs's arm lightly, briefly, and he felt the familiar blush flood his cheeks. This Alpha colony girl looked only a few years older than him, yet she had a wisdom about her that almost made her seem like an adult.

"Okay," Jobs said, taking a small step away from Echo and her serious brown eyes.

"There are many dangers out there. We have seen some from our observation station. And the Marauders tell us so."

"Okay," Jobs said again. "Uh, like what? Besides the flaming gas and all."

And, he added silently, *the awful, nagging scritching of little feet, always just out of sight. . . .*

Echo didn't answer him.

"Can you tell us what else to steer clear of?" Jobs asked, wondering if maybe he'd been unclear the first time.

Echo still remained silent. Instead her eyes darted to the Marauders gathered at the back of the low-ceilinged room.

Jobs got it. The other, unspoken dangers lay with the Marauders themselves. Jobs had seen that they were unpredictable and brutal. So, if there was more to watch out for, he and the others would have to be on their guard at all times.

Which would, no doubt, be easier said than done.

Jobs felt very, very tired. The last thing he wanted to do was to go to the Dark Zone. But he had to. For Mo'Steel.

Because Mo'Steel was his best friend. And because he was their only hope of survival.

The room stank. The whole place stank, every room and every corridor.

2Face was not happy to be here in this stinking underground hole. *More like a sewer,* she thought.

She didn't particularly relish the journey that lay ahead, but anything had to be better than being cooped up with these Alpha colony wackos.

Like that chick Echo. 2Face looked up from her task — packing a filthy bag with essentials for survival — and eyed Echo with suspicion.

That air of superiority. What was that about? Because her DNA had helped them to create a new life in their "lab"? 2Face snorted. This place was a joke. She looked up again. 2Face saw Echo offer something to Jobs, saw him take it, then give it back. *What's going on?* she wondered.

2Face did not like the way Echo favored Jobs.

We are in a mess, 2Face thought angrily, making a strong, tight knot in the ties of her pack. She just knew the Marauders and the Alphas were in on it. In on the plan not to let the people from the big ship survive any longer than necessary.

And she knew who was behind the whole thing. She knew the identity of the plot's supreme leader.

Billy.

It was all Billy's fault.

"Ow!" 2Face stumbled forward over the stack of rags at her feet. When she regained her footing, she turned around to see who had pushed her.

The Marauder named Nesia stood there, hands on her hips, grinning. "You are an ugly girl," she said through heavily cracked lips.

2Face was too furious to respond and just watched as Nesia swaggered away.

(CHAPTER TWO)

"NO ONE IS SPECIAL."

"Ouch!"

Mo'Steel sucked in a breath and bent, carefully, to pick up the small battered plate he'd just dropped. His torn thigh screamed with pain at the effort. *Just another inch,* he told himself. *Come on.* With the tips of his fingers Mo'Steel snatched up the plate and began the slow and painful rise to full height. When he finally got there his leg was actually shaking.

And the guy named Newton was looking at him like a lion looks at a limping gazelle. Mo'Steel knew he was going to need protection — a lot of it.

He looked away from the big Marauder and said loudly, "We're gonna need weapons."

The guy called Old Berg turned to the one-eared woman named Aga and grinned, but it wasn't a mean-spirited grin. Toothless, but not mean-spirited.

Then he turned back to Mo'Steel. "All Marauders carry weapons," he said, holding up his own crude club. "J'ou carry weapon, too. No one is special."

The woman named Nesia cackled and poked a little boy named Walbert, who, Echo had told him, was Nesia's son. Walbert edged away from his mother and looked up at Mo'Steel with curious eyes.

Duh. Of course everyone would carry his or her own weapon. Every man or woman for himself was probably the code of survival among these people. Mo'Steel wondered about the kids, though. You could arm a kid. But that didn't mean he or she could fight off a huge beast. Looking back at Walbert, who was pretty skinny, Mo'Steel wondered if Newton and the other strong ones would risk their lives to save one of their children.

He decided he didn't want to know the answer to that.

"Yeah," he said now, trying to bluster his way back to control. "Of course. What I meant was we want to choose what weapons we carry."

Aga nodded and poked Old Berg. The man turned and walked out of the room.

"Old Berg get j'ou some, j'ou wait," Aga said to him.

Mo'Steel nodded and, pretending his leg wasn't about to give out, he walked — pain pounding with every step — over to the closest wall and leaned back against it. He folded his arms across his chest and let his strong leg take as much weight off his wounded leg as it could.

Mo'Steel closed his eyes against the furtive looks of the Marauders and did some thinking.

Typical Marauder combat, Mo'Steel figured, was probably hand-to-hand, a fight-to-the-finish, kill-or-be-killed, one-man-left-standing sort of deal.

Like what had happened between Mo'Steel himself and big, bald Hawk.

Hawk had cut Mo'Steel with a crude, rusty knife that looked like it had been made from the lid off a can of tuna. Mo'Steel had seen other Marauders with similar makeshift weapons. Anything could be a weapon if the user's intent was strong.

And the Marauders had poison; Mo'Steel had heard that from an Alpha named Mattock. Back before the psychotropic storm, Hawk had destroyed Woody, the Alphas' leader, with a poisoned blade.

Mo'Steel opened his eyes. Old Berg was returning, lugging what looked like a dirty old pillowcase. He upturned the sack and spilled its contents at Mo'Steel's feet.

"Weapons," he grunted, panting slightly from the exertion. "J'ou choose."

Mo'Steel gritted his teeth and pushed carefully off the wall. He hadn't asked for the dubious honor of being next in line for leadership of the Marauders. *Man,* he thought, *I am not cut out to be a leader. That was more Jobs's sort of thing.*

Mo'Steel looked across to where his best buddy was fumbling with a huge knot in the strap of his pack, his face flushed. *Well,* he thought worriedly, *I gotta admit Jobs doesn't look much like leader material right now.*

When the Remnants were armed — except for Edward and Roger Dodger — Violet realized they were surrounded. The Alphas and Marauders stood in a two-person-deep semicircle around the Remnants.

But it didn't look like they were about to be attacked. In fact, it seemed the Marauders were about to conduct some sort of ceremony.

Violet listened as each Marauder formally introduced him- or herself. There was Newton, bigger than the others, a guy with a permanent look of suspicion or distrust. There were Claw and Snipe and Balder, only slightly smaller than Newton, but, Violet judged, looking at their dull eyes, far less intelligent. There was Rattler; from the way he swaggered around restlessly, Violet sensed he was trouble.

Old Berg seemed relatively harmless; maybe he just seemed tired. Then there was Cocker; he stood a bit apart from the other men and often glanced at Echo. A youngish guy named Eel stood next to Aga; she seemed to be the senior woman, formidable but not unkind. Violet had seen her alone with Old Berg and put them down as a couple.

Nesia — she was also trouble, Violet guessed; she was a bully. You could just tell by looking at her. A woman named Curia seemed unremarkable but for the fact that the Marauder children clustered around her. Yorka was introduced by Aga; Yorka didn't speak. Grost — she seemed sullen, Violet thought. Or maybe it was something else. . . .

Then there was a kid named Badger, maybe about Violet's own age. He had a receptive air about him, something open and curious that set him apart from the other Marauders. Violet decided she liked him.

Finally, there was Sanchez. Violet liked him, too, but she found that a bit troubling. He alone wore his hair shaved close to his scalp. He alone wore an adornment — a piece of metal strung on a cord and hanging down on his chest. There was something — otherworldly — about Sanchez. Violet thought it was like he was there in the room with them, powerful in presence, but also somewhere else — someplace she could not go.

"J'ou come from the sky," he said now, and it sounded more like a statement than a question.

Violet shot a glance at Olga, then at Jobs. Who was supposed to be the spokesperson? Mo'Steel?

"Well, uh, sort of," Jobs said.

"Don't lie!" Newton said sharply. "Marauders not stupid!" He took a step forward but was restrained by a look from Sanchez.

"As hard as this might be to understand," Violet said, modulating her voice to be gentle but not condescending, "we come from — the past."

And before Newton could explode again, she explained briefly how a handful of people had been selected to board the *Mayflower* just before the Rock hurtled into planet Earth, destroying everything.

Well, almost everything. Almost every*one*.

"For five hundred years we — existed — in a sort of coma," she said, watching the varied looks of puzzlement and suspicion and awe on the faces of Alphas and Marauders.

"And then," Jobs said suddenly, "we woke up. Some of us, anyway. Most of us were dead. We were on board a ship — the one you saw. An alien ship."

"What j'ou mean, alien?" Newton said, eyes narrowed.

"People — creatures — exist throughout the universe, not just here on Earth," Jobs explained. "Life-forms far more advanced than humans — I mean, than humans like us, like those of us before the Rock. See —"

Violet registered the rising fury of the Alphas and Marauders and knew she had to shut Jobs up in order to prevent a fight.

"Long story short," she said hurriedly, "there was trouble. Lots of it. And then some — people — took the ship and left us stranded here. With you. Except we didn't know you were here."

"What were j'ou doing here in the first place?" Westie demanded. She was the first Alpha to have joined the conversation. "How did j'ou find us? Did j'ou know this was Earth?"

"We looked for you," Jobs said. "For Earth, I

mean. We hoped — we wanted to come back. We hoped we could find a home here."

"Earth is not j'our home!" That was an Alpha named Ali Kosh.

"But it used to be," Olga said, sounding like she was going to cry.

"Then why did j'ou leave when it was threatened?" Westie asked.

"How could we stay?" Olga looked at Violet as if for assurance. "How could we fight?"

"We stayed," Old Berg said. "We fought, in our own way. Our forefathers and mothers."

Some of us were just kids, Violet said silently to herself. *Some of us still are.*

"This place doesn't belong to j'ou," Rattler snarled.

"Are you saying we can't stay?!" 2Face demanded. "How the heck are we supposed to leave? Where are we supposed to go?!"

Violet felt her stomach clench.

"J'ou pose a severe threat to our resources. J'ou are an unknown quantity in a world in which every factor must be carefully assessed. And some of us still question j'our story."

"Then why are you letting us stay?" Violet asked, looking imploringly at Sanchez, dreading the answer but wanting to know. "Why does Mo'Steel have to fight these Beasts? Why?"

"It is enough that j'ou are alive," Sanchez said with finality. "Answers will come in time."

Old Berg stepped forward into the center of the circle and pointed to a pile of what looked like skin pouches.

"Here," he said. "Each of j'ou will take one. J'ou will keep it close. If j'ou lose it, there is no more. It is a sign that j'ou be a Marauder."

"For now," Newton muttered.

Violet gently shoved Mo'Steel forward. He should be the first to take a bladder.

She watched as he bent to grab the closest bladder. She knew him well enough to see the extreme pain he was trying to mask. When he stood his face was gray.

Violet's heart sank.

CHAPTER THREE

"WHAT DID I EVER DO TO HER?"

Nice, 2Face thought, fingering the cruddy bladder into which the last of her precious water had been trickled. *Now I have a purse to match my outfit. If anyone thinks I'm actually going to drink from this thing . . .*

Something made her raise her head, some noise or maybe a change in the air — an increase in tension. 2Face hadn't thought that was possible, but obviously, she'd been wrong. Facing 2Face and the other Remnant females, in a tight bunch of smelly rags and skins, were the Marauder females.

"Where is j'our babies?" the old woman demanded suddenly.

Before 2Face could reply, "It's none of your business," Olga stepped forward. "These girls," she said, gesturing to Violet and Noyze and lastly to 2Face, "are too young to be mothers. Um, where we come from."

The Marauder women didn't seem to like Olga's answer. Some snickered. One gave 2Face and the other girls the once-over and laughed. The old woman glared at the other Marauder women and they quieted down.

"And j'ou?" she said to Olga.

Olga pointed to Mo'Steel.

"He's my son," she said calmly, though 2Face could see a blush rising on her cheeks. "You know that already."

"Others?" the old woman persisted.

2Face rolled her eyes. What was the point of all these questions?

"No others," Olga replied. "He's my only child."

There was a moment of tense silence. 2Face itched with annoyance. But then the old woman relaxed her frowning expression and smiled. Sort of.

"I am Aga," she said.

"Yes," Olga replied. "I know. I am Olga."

The similarity of the two names seemed to strike the woman as a good omen or something because she opened her mouth and actually laughed. The others took her cue and smiled and one touched Noyze's hair and another shoved a little kid at Violet, who knelt and went all goopy over him.

Everyone seemed suddenly all okay except for 2Face — and the monster called Nesia.

Nesia was a big woman, taller than 2Face by a good four inches and, in spite of a lean and paltry diet, strong. 2Face wouldn't have been surprised to learn that Nesia was stealing food from her own kid. Walbert looked a little too skinny for long-term survival.

And Nesia was mean. Not very bright but very mean. You could tell that from a mile away.

While Olga and Aga were bonding, Nesia pushed her way through the other Marauder women. 2Face stood her ground as Nesia swaggered up to her. The big woman stopped only two feet from 2Face and sneered.

"J'ou don't even have baby," Nesia said, spitting on the bunker's concrete floor. The spittle made a tiny circle on the ground and then seemed to be sucked away, even the hard floor of the bunker desperate for what moisture it could get.

Aga made a harsh, angry sound and suddenly, the group of women went silent. 2Face was the center of attention.

"So? What's so great about having a kid?" 2Face knew a fight when she saw one coming. This freak was pushing her buttons.

Nesia stepped closer and laughed. Involuntarily, 2Face flinched from the girl's rancid smell.

"J'ou is ugly. J'ou is worthless Marauder woman."

"You're a disgusting freak," 2Face said between clenched teeth.

Nesia laughed loudly and swaggered away. The other Marauder women followed her, but not before eyeing 2Face with — what was that look? Concern? Suspicion?

Dumb as a bucket of rocks, 2Face thought. It wasn't bad enough they were stuck with this band of mutants. Oh, no. 2Face had to have her own personal enemy, just to make the nasty scenario complete.

"What did I ever do to her?" she muttered.

"You shouldn't have egged her on," Olga whispered harshly. "You're always causing trouble."

"What?"

"You might have put us in danger," Violet said now. "We don't need any more fighting."

"Yeah," Noyze added. "Just do us a favor and stay away from her, okay?"

2Face looked back at the thin, tired, and intent faces looking at her and felt a tiny flicker of fear. Was it really possible they would abandon her if she messed things up with Nesia?

The blood rushed to 2Face's head.

And Billy, where is Billy? she thought wildly as Olga, Violet, and Noyze turned away from her, too. Somewhere out there, somewhere in that bleak landscape. Oh, yeah. Billy was somewhere out there watching and waiting, biding his time until he struck and killed them all.

Maybe it would be better to be dead, 2Face thought, then violently rejected the idea. *No.*

Nesia wasn't the real problem, after all. Billy was.

Jobs pretended to be totally focused on gearing up, but he was really just as busy sizing up the competition. The Marauders. Especially the Marauder males.

As Jobs saw it, Newton was their main worry.

Newton was big, maybe six feet tall and with shoulders any pre-Rock linebacker would have been proud of. And, he was very smart. Jobs could see right off that Newton had the look of a man who chose craft over grasping, bullish behavior to get what he wanted. Still, Jobs had no doubt that if craft didn't work, Newton would easily resort to violence.

Jobs snuck a look at Newton. Newton's face was one of the least scarred and deformed. Its worst offense was a large nose that had been broken at least once and left unmended. A pre-Rock Newton — if that could even be imagined — might have been a decent-looking guy, the kind of big, handsome athletic type who goes into corporate life after a major college football career and makes a ton of money.

As if he'd heard Jobs thinking about him, Newton suddenly glanced keen-eyed around the room. His gaze quickly settled on Jobs.

Jobs looked away. After a moment or two, he snuck another look at the corner where Newton had been working. What he saw there now made his blood run cold.

Newton was staring at Violet in a way that made Jobs extremely nervous. Jobs's heart began to pound. How were he and Mo'Steel supposed to go up against guys whose major form of recreation seemed to be brawling?

And even if Newton exhibited some self-restraint, what about the crude, lumpish guys who formed his posse? Snipe, Claw, and Balder might not be as smart as Newton but they were even bigger, which put Jobs at a serious disadvantage. Smart he could combat. Stupid, that just put him at a loss.

Maybe, he thought, *maybe they'll all actually obey Mo'Steel as their leader and maybe we won't have to fight them off.*

Jobs looked at the guy named Claw. He was busy picking something from his crude vest of stitched-together skins; then he was busy chewing on the something.

Yeah, Jobs thought dispiritedly. *Maybe.*

Violet adjusted the rough straps of her pack. Already the skin on her shoulders was blistering.

It was time to move out.

The motley crew was loaded down with packs and stuff banded to and slung across their bodies, stuff like the beast bladders full of stale water — where did the Marauders get the water, anyway? — and those stuffed with food that rightly belonged to the Alphas.

Violet sighed and made a quick check of her other gear. She still had her flashlight. She wanted to check the batteries but was keenly aware that with every flick of the switch she was wasting power. Violet wanted the flashlight to be ready to roll when they reached the Dark Zone. *If* they reached the Dark Zone.

"What do you think is going to happen?"

It was D-Caf.

"D-Caf," Violet answered wearily, "I have no idea."

The kid had something else he wanted to say, though. Violet could see it in his wide, frightened eyes.

"What?" she said.

D-Caf hunched in closer to Violet and spoke in a too-low voice.

"Do you think . . . um —"

"Come on. What?" Violet snapped.

D-Caf touched her arm with a fingertip, then quickly withdrew the finger.

"Do you think maybe we'll have to go worm?" he whispered. "I don't want to ever do that again."

Violet shot a glance at those closest to them. No one seemed to be listening. *Me either,* she thought. Her cheeks, she just knew, had gone pale.

"Violet?"

Violet looked away from the boy who was too much like her for comfort. The boy who shared her — mutation.

"Please keep your mouth shut about that," she said, and walked away.

CHAPTER FOUR

NOTHING BUT OUR WITS WILL
PROTECT US THEN.

The band of Remnants and Marauders, led by a limping Mo'Steel, moved out. None of the Alphas who stood watching them file out of the bunker said a word.

But Echo caught Jobs's eye and she waved to him. The girl who stood with her, Lyric, smiled and put her hand to her mouth coyly. The woman named Westie frowned.

As soon as Jobs's feet touched the ashy ground of planet Earth, his heart sank further than it ever had. He wondered if everyone else who'd been left behind by Yago felt as low and without hope as he did.

Jobs supposed he should be amazed that he was alive. He had been certain he and the others would die of starvation — if thirst didn't kill them first —

while stranded on Earth's arid surface. Stumbling across the Alpha colony had been a lucky thing, hadn't it? In some ways, at least. And so was the fact that Mo'Steel just happened to kill the right Marauder. That was seriously lucky.

But Jobs just couldn't feel upbeat about anything. Not now. Not yet. He glanced around at the others. No one was talking. There was an air of solemnity to the band. Jobs wondered how long it would last.

He wished he knew. Especially in a situation like this, where very little — if anything — was stable, Jobs needed to be sure. Even after the debacle of his failed experiment and Yago's treachery, Jobs clung to his scientific nature. It was who he was.

But all Jobs could be sure of now were a few minor facts. Like the fact that the Remnants had lost most of their stuff in the fury of the storm and their ensuing capture. Still, they had a few things left.

Jobs had a spade stuck in his belt. The Alphas hadn't confiscated it; seems they had enough instruments of cultivation to last them another twenty-five generations.

Jobs brought his mind back to facts. "What else do we have?" he muttered.

As for the fifty-six feet of rope the group had

carried among them, thirty feet of it was still intact. Ten had gone with Anamull; nothing of Anamull's had survived D-Caf's attack. Another sixteen feet of rope had just — gone.

The forty-eight crackers that had been distributed among the group had met a varied fate. Four had gone away with Anamull.

Thirty-eight crackers had been eaten or lost. And the six that Jobs had carried in the pocket of his jacket had been taken by the Alphas. First by the elders, for analysis. Then by Echo.

Echo had tried to return the crumbly crackers just before he'd set out with the others on this quest. But Jobs had given them back to her, mumbled something about her being hungry.

Echo had seemed confused by his offer but ultimately had taken them.

"You eat them yourself, okay?" Jobs had said.

Jobs sighed and wondered about Echo. But his mind slipped inevitably back to the comfort of facts.

The gun he'd had? Gone. Lost or stolen, Jobs didn't know which. And the Rider sword? Also gone.

Jobs suddenly jumped up and looked behind him. He thought he heard the sound of those scritching little feet. He whirled around but again, nothing was there.

Nothing that he could see, anyway. Nothing but the surly face of Claw and the dull face of Grost, bobbing along side by side.

Jobs shuddered and turned face front. He wondered if Echo was watching him from the Alphas' observation post.

He wondered who else was watching him.

How long had it been? How long since they'd left the Alpha colony and started out on their trek?

We're refugees, Olga thought. *And we're heading for a place that . . . a place that will probably kill us, if the Beasts don't first.*

This grim thought brought to Olga an awareness of a headache forming behind her eyes, low and dim on the horizon, but steadily growing nearer.

Great, she thought, *now this.* None of the Remnants had aspirin. And Olga did not want to chance taking any form of pain relief the Marauders might have. She had a strong feeling that anything used by these people might kill her flat out.

Olga rolled her neck and willed the pain to stop its advance. The result was a flash behind her right eye that almost knocked her to her knees.

"Mom?"

It was Mo'Steel, suddenly at her side. He took her elbow and whispered, "Are you okay?"

Olga forced a smile and said, "Yes, I'm fine. Sorry. I just tripped."

Mo'Steel eyed her with doubt but let go of her elbow.

"Why don't you talk to Noyze?" she suggested. "See how she's doing. And then shouldn't you be up front? They'll expect you to be in the lead. It's important you be strong."

Her son nodded and walked ahead. Olga sighed. Best not to tell anyone she was getting sick, she thought. Best just to keep quiet.

Focus on something else, Olga told herself. So she forced herself to pay attention to the surroundings and to the people with whom she was traveling. The more she knew about the Marauders — the enemy? — the better.

Like the fact that the Marauders were practiced nomads. In spite of carrying their entire worldly possessions on their backs, the Marauders moved swiftly and surely through the gray shadowy stretches.

No two ways about it, Olga thought. *We need them if we're going to survive. At least until we get to the land of the Beasts. Nothing but our wits will protect us then.*

* * *

Violet was thirsty.

The clawing need for water . . . Thirst was maddening in a way that hunger could never be, Violet thought, licking her dry, cracked lips and making no difference at all. After a while, the stomach got used to being empty. But the throat and skin and blood and muscles never, ever got used to being parched. Violet had read somewhere that it took only a few days to die of dehydration.

Well, it wasn't that the Marauders had no water to drink. It was that they'd been conditioned since birth to survive on amazingly small quantities of water. In fact, Violet wondered if the Marauders even knew what real thirst was. She decided to ask one of the less fierce Marauders someday. Maybe.

In the meantime, Violet vowed to try to stop thinking about cold bottles of sparkling water and icy cans of cola. *That way lies madness,* she told herself. *And there's enough of that here already.*

(CHAPTER FIVE)

IT WAS NO PLACE FOR THE LIVING.

Noyze kicked lightly at ashy ground as she walked. She liked to watch the top layer of loose ash billow gently around her feet.

It was almost pretty. Almost.

"You okay?" Mo'Steel asked, walking up beside her.

No, Noyze thought, *not really.* But she said, "Yeah, I'm okay. You know."

"Yeah. I know."

"How's your leg? Is the infection clearing up?"

"A little," Mo'Steel said. "Slowly."

"I wish I could do something to help. I wish we had enough water, hot water. You could soak your leg. . . ." Noyze trailed off, embarrassingly aware of how silly it was to wish for the impossible.

It was just that things now were so — hard. And disgusting. There was no Billy. And . . .

And then there was the dirt and the stench that went along with the endless walking. The Marauders simply didn't wash. How could they, with the little water they had all reserved for consumption?

Noyze had noticed that the Alphas hadn't seemed bothered by the Marauders' smells. Maybe that was because the Alphas didn't smell so sweet, either. Or maybe the Alphas were only pretending so as not to offend the Marauders and start a fight the Alphas knew they could not win.

"Noyze?"

Mo'Steel's voice startled Noyze back to the moment and to the guy she cared about, standing right beside her.

"You okay?" he said. "You just stopped talking and your eyes got kind of sad all of a sudden."

Noyze managed a smile. "Yeah," she said. "Sorry. I was just — thinking about things."

"We'll manage somehow," Mo'Steel said.

Noyze really appreciated him for his hope. At least, for his pretending to hope, for her sake.

"I know," she said, taking his hurt hand gently. "I believe you."

* * *

D-Caf had something on his mind. He scurried ahead to catch up with Violet and Noyze, who were now keeping pace.

"Hey, guys? What happens if there's another one of those dream storms?" D-Caf asked fearfully. "The Marauders could freak out while we're all hallucinating. We'll be helpless!"

"Maybe not," Noyze said. "Remember, Mo'Steel accidentally killed that guy Hawk while he was hallucinating."

Violet sighed loudly. "Yeah, but not all of us are Mo'Steel."

"True." Noyze considered. "I wonder how the Marauders stand it. Maybe they have a trick or something. A way of blocking out the effects of the storm."

"Maybe. But are you going to ask them to share their little trick with us?" Violet said.

Noyze frowned. "No."

D-Caf shook his head worriedly and thought about those horrible worms inside him.

Violet looked over her shoulder at D-Caf. He'd fallen behind again and was talking to himself. Or to the ghosts.

This place is way too crowded, Violet thought.

Planet Earth was the home of seven billion ghosts. Seven billion ghosts who seemed to linger and watch and hiss their deep, long discontent as the survivors of the Rock made their precarious way across the desert of the Shadow Zone and on into the frozen wastes of the Dark Zone.

No doubt about it, Violet thought. Earth was no place for the living.

CHAPTER SIX

SOMETHING DEFINITELY WAS NOT NORMAL.

The first "night" passed without incident. Mo'Steel surprised himself by sleeping soundly and rising with an appetite for pancakes.

Trouble was, there were no pancakes for breakfast, only a handful of twigs. *Not even a berry,* he thought sadly.

When the band had geared up, Mo'Steel did what they were waiting for him to do. He felt like an idiot; he didn't even know in which direction they were supposed to be walking. But he was the leader, so he raised his right hand high and made a sort of "ho!" noise. Newton scowled — *nothing new there,* Mo'Steel thought — and nodded in a general direction. Jobs shot Mo'Steel a half-smile of commiseration and everybody moved out, walking behind Mo'Steel and then Newton, Claw, and Snipe.

It wasn't until they had gone some way and

Mo'Steel had walked back through the band check-ing for — whatever — that he noticed there was something wrong. Mo'Steel rubbed more sleep from his eyes — coffee would have been nice, too — and tried to focus.

And then he saw it.

Aga. On her head she wore the shapeless piece of cloth that had passed for Old Berg's hat.

What was Old Berg wearing, then?

"You see that?" Jobs whispered, coming up be-side him. "You see what Newton's carrying? It's Old Berg's club, I'm sure of it."

Mo'Steel nodded. "And Old Berg's woman is wearing his hat. Question is: Where's Old Berg gone to?"

Jobs looked troubled. "Maybe we should — ask someone?"

"Hey, Newton," Mo'Steel called. From his place near the head of the band Newton halted, and everybody halted with him.

Right, like I'm ever going to be the real leader, Mo'Steel thought. *Who are we all kidding?*

Mo'Steel walked up to Newton, aware that Jobs followed him a few paces behind.

"Where's Old Berg?" he said, including Aga in his questioning glance.

Aga looked to Newton.

"He's been sick for some time," Newton said, then grunted. "Nothing else to do. It's Old Berg's choice to stay behind now. J'ou got trouble with this?"

Yes, thought Mo'Steel, *I do have trouble with this.*

"He's going to die," he said, knowing, of course, that dying was what Old Berg had set out to do.

Mo'Steel flashed a glance at his mother and felt a chill run up his spine. He'd seen the signs — the paleness, the squinting eyes, the stumbling. He knew she was getting a seriously bad migraine. And he knew that even if he made it out of this nightmare alive, his mother might not.

Newton laughed and fondled Old Berg's club. "Old Berg be dead by now maybe. What j'ou going to do about it?"

Mo'Steel was torn. He knew he couldn't reverse what had been decided by Old Berg and probably by Newton, as well. But he also knew he couldn't just walk on and leave the old man without at least saying good-bye.

He's one of my people now, isn't he? Mo'Steel thought. *I'm supposed to be his leader. Don't I owe him some sign of respect at the end?*

Yeah, he decided, *I do.*

35

"You go on," Mo'Steel said, hoping his voice sounded commanding. "I'm going back to say good-bye to Old Berg. I'll catch up with you."

There was a sudden hush, loud in its stunned silence.

Newton glanced at his comrades, Snipe and Claw and Balder, each in turn. When he turned back to Mo'Steel, he was grinning.

But before he could speak, Aga, Old Berg's woman, grabbed Mo'Steel's arm, hard.

"J'ou don't go back there," she said fiercely. "J'ou bring shame on Old Berg. He was a good man, j'ou leave him be."

"But he has no food, no water, no weapons," Noyze protested. "What chance does he have?"

"J'ou stupid," Newton said, and bared his rotted teeth. "Old Berg, he got no chance. If bad thirst don't get Old Berg, Beasts or Savagers or the big flames will kill him. Old Berg is as good as dead and I got his club."

Mo'Steel shook free of Aga's grip.

"Savagers? Who are they?" he said.

Yorka, the mute one, made an inarticulate moan and Mo'Steel knew for sure that the Savagers were seriously bad news.

"J'ou our leader, right? It's the leader's duty to

keep Marauders safe from Savagers," Newton said, baring his nasty teeth. "Maybe j'ou kill them, eh?"

"Yeah," Mo'Steel said, trying for bravado, "maybe I will."

Newton snickered and turned away.

Mo'Steel walked back to the front of the band. He felt sick. He wasn't stupid. He knew that the Remnants were a big drain on the Marauders' food and water supply. Old Berg had done the honorable thing for everyone by taking himself out of the picture.

It made Mo'Steel feel rotten. He knew he was being tested at every turn and he knew he was largely failing the Marauders' tests.

And if I fail completely, he thought, *I fail Jobs and Mom and Noyze and . . .*

Mo'Steel sucked up his self-doubts and said in a loud voice, "Let's go."

Mo'Steel set a good pace and kept his eyes on the terrain ahead. After about five minutes he glanced over his shoulder.

Okay, he thought. *They're following. For now.*

Jobs watched Edward and Eel talking animatedly as they walked. Eel was Aga's son with Old Berg. Jobs wondered how Eel felt about his father's being left behind.

Old Berg. *Okay,* Jobs thought, *the guy had defi-nitely seen better days, but — old?* Forty was Jobs's guess. Certainly not old by pre-Rock standards. But in this brutal, postapocalyptic world? Forty was an-cient.

It was almost impossible to tell the age of any given Marauder, but Jobs found that it was possible to place them in relation to one another. Eel seemed younger than Newton and his cronies, but older than the guy called Badger. Jobs placed Eel at about nine-teen or twenty. Old enough to be a sort of surro-gate father figure to Edward, only six.

And I'm only his big brother, Jobs thought, suddenly angry and jealous and suspicious.

The feelings took him by surprise. They worried him. He'd never been paranoid before. What was happening to him?

It's this place, Jobs told himself, trudging on. *It gets to you.*

A shrill cry of laughter met his ears. Jobs jumped, then saw it had come from the children, all walking in a pack, Prota carrying Tackie on her back.

The little kids: Tackie, a toddler; Walbert, maybe five; Prota, a bit older; Micron, Walbert's particular buddy, also about five; and Croce, older than the others, maybe about ten.

And then there were Edward and Roger Dodger. Already they seemed pretty comfortable with the other kids, though Edward hadn't gone chameleon since they'd all hooked up, probably because he was naturally a little shy, especially around older kids. Croce, the oldest of the bunch — except for Roger Dodger, who was essentially an outsider — pushed the others around a bit but that was normal, wasn't it?

Yeah, it is, Jobs decided. *But what isn't normal is . . .*

Jobs couldn't say, exactly. He looked fearfully over his shoulder.

Something definitely was not normal.

Olga's head felt like it was exploding.

Please, please stop, she cried silently, because opening her mouth to talk or to sob would just make her more ill, just invite the meager contents of her stomach to fling themselves upon the ashy ground.

Vaguely, through eyes almost entirely shut against the dim but excruciatingly painful light, Olga saw someone. . . .

"Mom, it's me. I know you're sick, don't tell me you're not."

Mo'Steel touched her arm and Olga flinched.

Her nerve endings were hypersensitive; her skin was a punishment.

"Mom, let me carry your pack for a while. No one will notice, I promise."

Through the violence of the migraine Olga's maternal instincts cried out. *No.* It was bad enough her son had to walk on that infected leg. She wouldn't burden him further. Besides, Mo'Steel's carrying her pack would not go unnoticed. It would signal to the Marauders loud and clear that something was wrong, that she was sick and weak. That thought frightened Olga. She didn't really want to die alone in this place. And who would be there for her son if she was gone?

Ignoring her son's whispered pleas, Olga stumbled on. Every step was agony. She just wanted to sit down.

But she wouldn't.

Noyze. That was her voice. . . .

"Maybe I could rub your neck or something. . . ."

Oh, why won't they all leave me alone? Olga signed her refusal. She appreciated the offer but knew that the merest touch would exacerbate the agony, send her hurtling into deeper dizziness.

Maybe they should leave me behind, Olga thought now, taking another agonizing step. *Like Old Berg, maybe my time is up.*

* * *

How glamorous the term "road trip" sounds, Noyze thought. How cool. A convertible car, a handsome boyfriend, the wind in your hair.

Noyze sighed and lay back, her head on her pack as a pillow. *This is no glamorous road trip,* she thought. *No way, nohow.* At least nothing terrible had happened yet. No one had died and there hadn't been any big fights, at least that Noyze knew about.

Someone was already snoring. Noyze was annoyed. She could never sleep when someone was snoring. Her father used to snore and even though her parents' bedroom was all the way down the hall from hers, it kept her awake at night. Noyze turned onto her stomach . . .

And it was there. It was standing not ten feet from her, hollow-eyed, accusing, wanting retribution.

Noyze screamed and the scream morphed almost immediately into a long, low whimper.

It's looking at me, make it stop looking at me, she begged silently. *Oh, please, please.*

Noyze hid her face in the folds of her dusty tunic, like a child hiding under the covers from the bogeyman.

She felt hands on her, hands, but . . .

"What is it? Come on, I'm here now. It's Violet."

Violet's hands, not . . .

"A . . . a ghost," Noyze whispered. "A . . . a man who used to live here. Before. Before the Rock. He . . . was staring at me. He was angry. He . . . he had no hands."

"No one's here but me," Violet soothed. "Just try to calm down."

"He pointed the stumps of his arms at me. He said, he said it was my fault. . . ."

Noyze felt Violet's hands tighten on her shoulders and felt both horrified and reassured.

"It's my fault they all died," she crooned. "It's my fault."

"What's going on?"

"Mo'Steel . . ." Noyze murmured.

And then she heard another voice, a harsh one, the voice of a man, ask, "What's wrong with her?"

"Nothing, she's fine. We're just talking."

That was Violet.

"It's under control," Mo'Steel said now, and he sounded very sure. "She's fine. Go back to sleep."

"We have to be on our way before long. If she—"

"I *said* she's fine."

Mo'Steel's angry voice frightened Noyze but some instinct made her keep her mouth shut.

Shuffling footsteps, followed by silence. Then:

"A hallucination," Violet said softly. "Something like what happened with the storm. She'll come out of it."

"Let me stay with her. You go rest. And don't tell anyone else about this."

Noyze felt Violet's hands go away. Then she felt Mo'Steel's arms go around her and she turned her face into his chest, wanting to bury it there so the man with no hands and the man with the harsh voice couldn't find her. . . .

"You're going to be okay," Mo'Steel whispered into her hair.

"Lies," Noyze chanted. "Lies, lies, lies."

CHAPTER SEVEN

"LET IT GO, DUCK."

They were ready to move on again. The pain in Olga's head had receded enough to allow her to think somewhat clearly. The freedom felt wonderful.

"You know," she said to Violet, "if we make it out of this alive, maybe someday I'll write a definitive study of the Alpha colony and the Marauders. I could do it. I know enough about scientific principle and research methods."

Violet laughed. "And who would read it?"

Olga shrugged her pack into a more comfortable position. "Oh," she said. "I hadn't thought of that. Maybe I'll just write it for me. As a personal project."

Violet sighed. "You're a better person than I am, Olga."

Am I? Olga wondered.

"Inbreeding."

"Huh?"

"Inbreeding," Violet repeated. "I was thinking about inbreeding. You'd have to talk about that in your book."

Yeah, she would. Olga glanced at the Marauders around her. No doubt some of their — irregularities — were caused by inbreeding. It caused genetic defects to surface with greater frequency than they might occur in a larger, more varied population.

"Remember that self-important Alpha woman named Westie?" she asked Violet.

"Sure." Violet laughed. "She reminded me of my mother."

"She told me the Alphas were carefully guarding against inbreeding by a studied distribution of genetic material."

"Where'd they get the, er, genetic material?" Violet asked.

"Actually, it was stolen by the founders of the underground biosphere before the Rock, just in case people did survive. They knew that in a world with a tiny population, genetic diversity would be key to continued survival."

"Smart," Violet commented. "Illegal, but smart."

Olga and Violet walked on in companionable silence for a while. Olga watched and listened. Curia was fondly smoothing her little girl's hair. Croce was chasing Micron; both boys' voices were shrill with excitement. Walbert shouted with glee when Croce finally caught Micron and the two boys tumbled laughingly to the ground.

Olga smiled. "The Marauders seem — almost carefree."

"What do you mean?"

"Well," Olga said, "Westie told me the children aren't planned for, like they are with the Alphas."

"Olga? What happens if Echo's baby is born with some genetic defect?" Violet asked. "It could happen, right? Even with all the precautions?"

"I don't know," Olga admitted.

Olga adjusted her pack and resisted the desire to rub her temples. They passed Aga, who was moving slowly.

With the loss of Old Berg, Aga was the oldest Marauder. With her missing ear and dark skin scored with threadlike scars, Olga put Aga at a very worn thirty-five.

Violet seemed to be reading Olga's thoughts. "The Marauder women," she said when they were out of Aga's hearing, "seem to age so much more rapidly than the men."

"Yeah," Olga agreed. "Not surprising, given their harsh lifestyle."

"Some of the Alphas looked pretty old. I mean, older than the oldest Marauders but healthier," Violet said.

"Yes." Olga thought. "For one, they're largely protected from certain detrimental environmental factors such as —"

"Such as the Beasts," Violet said abruptly.

The words brought a stab of pain and Olga winced.

"I'm sorry," Violet said. "Are you okay?"

"I'm fine," Olga lied.

"No, you're not," Violet countered. "You're my friend, Olga. When the pain gets too bad I'll tell Mo'Steel. He'll call a rest. So, don't lie to me, okay? We're in this together."

Olga felt tears come to her eyes and didn't know if they were tears of joy or sadness.

Jobs had wandered off a bit. He had the band in full view, so it wasn't like he was going to get lost. He just needed to be alone for a while, not too long. Too many ghosts.

Jobs spotted something off about five yards to

his right. It wasn't a big something but anything on the surface of this particular stretch of barren land stood out.

Curiosity took over. Jobs set out to take a closer look at whatever it was that made a bump on the land.

A few minutes later Jobs stood over the bump. Unmistakable. It was the small withered body of a Meanie. The suit was nowhere in sight. At a glance, there was no evidence of the injury that had felled the Meanie — if there ever had been. Maybe the Meanie had died of — thirst? Or the lack of some other life-supporting substance essential to Meanies.

Anamull had destroyed two Meanies and here was a third one dead. That left one Meanie and two Riders unaccounted for.

Jobs wondered if he should call out and tell the Marauders what he'd found. But then he couldn't think of a reason why they should know or why they should care. And maybe knowing that there were aliens possibly still alive on their planet would freak them out. Maybe it would make them turn on Mo'Steel and Jobs and the others.

"Let it go, Duck."

Jobs felt his heart leap to his mouth. "I didn't hear you," he said when he caught his breath.

Mo'Steel put an arm around Jobs's shoulders. Jobs let himself be pulled away from the dead Meanie.

"They weren't so bad, the Meanies," Jobs said. "Not all of them, anyway."

"Every group has its good guys and its bad," his friend agreed. "Let's catch up with the others."

Mo'Steel had called a halt. Newton had grumbled about losing time but Mo'Steel had stood his ground. Olga and some of the others were sleeping but Violet was restless.

She paced through their temporary camp, alone and watching. The Marauders puzzled her, though she was trying to understand more about them all the time. *Knowledge is power,* Violet reminded herself.

Prota ran by, giggling. Tackie waddled along behind, trying to catch up.

Violet smiled.

Marauder children were often happy. She'd seen them playing a variety of games. Some of the younger ones even carried crude dolls, mini versions of their wild and tattered selves.

Violet strolled toward some of the boys, including Edward and Roger Dodger. Roger Dodger was teaching Walbert and the others how to play marbles with a motley collection of small, roughly spherical objects. Croce scored and let out a whoop of triumph.

"The young ones enjoy their games."

Violet started. It was Sanchez. He moved up next to her and nodded at the children.

"The young ones are the future. The old must make way for the young. They must know when to give their lives for the healthy and strong."

"Like Old Berg," Violet said.

Sanchez smiled a slight smile and said, "Yes. J'ou are one of the wise of j'our people."

Violet couldn't help but laugh and felt a blush rise to her cheeks. Sanchez's compliment was absurd — but it pleased her, too. She stole a glance at him and noticed, suddenly, the regularity of his profile and the length of his dark eyelashes.

Quickly, Violet looked away and back to the children. The strength of her feelings had startled her.

Hold on, she berated herself silently. *The last thing you need is to get goopy over some wild guy. Even if he is probably the most handsome and intelligent of the Marauders. Remember, Violet. The guy can't read!*

They stood in silence for a moment. Violet wanted to say something, anything, but no words would come. And then Sanchez broke the silence.

"Some of j'our people are weak," he said.

Violet was at a loss for words again. Instead she made a small sound, inviting him to go on.

"The weak are bad for us. Why is it that j'our leader favors the weak? This will not last. Some Marauders will not let this go on."

"Are you threatening us?" Violet demanded, all soft feelings for Sanchez gone, anger and fear battling for control of her. *Olga and her headache. Noyze and the hallucinations. All of us with mutations. Mo'Steel with his injured leg . . .*

Sanchez looked at her calmly, almost without expression, much as he'd spoken.

"I am warning j'ou," he said.

Violet stood trembling as Sanchez shuffled off into the dust.

Newton rambled through the temporary camp, alert to the activities of everyone, watching for rebellion. . . .

"Why he always stopping?"

It was Claw. He was agitated, his facial tics worse than usual, his hand on his knife.

"I think he no want to get to them Beasts, all right. Big leader be scared!"

Newton didn't answer right away, which seemed

to make Claw more excited. "He scared and he trying to protect that woman, Olga. She be sick, I see it!"

"Calm down," Newton commanded, voice tight. Balder and Snipe were striding toward them, their faces dark. He had to keep control.

"We should be moving on," Balder said as the two men reached Newton.

"Why we not lead the kid in the wrong direction and just leave him?" Snipe growled.

The idea had occurred to Newton, too. But Sanchez had warned him to follow tradition. And he'd said something else, something Newton didn't understand, about an "event coming to pass." Sanchez's words had scared Newton — a little. Sanchez knew things.

"No," Newton said harshly now. "We will take them all to the Beasts."

Balder shifted his protruding eyes to Snipe, and Newton's hands clenched.

"J'ou hear me?" he demanded. "J'ou leave them all alone unless I say so."

Newton waited for one of the men to argue and when none did, he moved on through the camp. The minor confrontation had been unsettling and Newton needed to be alone.

He didn't like that the kid named Mo'Steel had managed to kill Hawk.

Now Hawk was gone and Newton — who'd always thought he'd be next in line for leader, even if it meant he'd have to kill Hawk, who was, by the way, his older brother — Newton was supposed to follow this kid from the past, a coward who'd run off when things got tough.

Well, that wasn't going to happen. Not if Newton had anything to do with it. Yes, Newton thought, striding showily now, wanting the weak to fear him, wanting to impress, *I'm going to guide them to the Beasts because it's tradition, like Sanchez said.*

Newton stumbled and cursed. He knew people had seen him and humiliation quickly turned into rage. He wanted to hurt somebody for having witnessed his weakness. Grost was close by, and as he passed her, he gave her a shove. She cried out, spilling the bundle she'd been clutching.

Newton grinned. It helped mask the uneasy knowledge that there was another reason he was holding off on killing Mo'Steel outright. If he did, then he, Newton, would have to fight the Beasts before being acknowledged the Marauders' leader.

Newton could hardly acknowledge it to himself but he was afraid of the Beasts.

Yeah, so he'd guide them all to the Dark Zone and wait for the Beasts to come. But he wouldn't make the trip too easy. No, he'd let Mo'Steel and his people survive but he'd make it hard.

And when the Beasts had gotten rid of the kid, Newton would declare himself leader and just see who had the nerve to argue with him.

Newton came to a stop and surveyed the camp's activities. Grost was still sprawled on the ground. Aga was bending over her. The Olga woman was lying with her face hidden in her arms. Mo'Steel was replacing the dirty bandage on his leg. Claw, Snipe, and Balder had followed Newton and now came to his side.

Suddenly, the girl called 2Face cried out and they saw her break away from Rattler, a big grin on his greasy face.

"You guys are disgusting!" she shouted.

Newton clenched his hands into fists at his side.

"J'ou hear that?" Claw growled. "J'ou hear what that one say about Marauders?"

Snipe reached for his knife but Newton stopped him with a glance.

"The Marauders will have respect," Newton said. "J'ou with me? We will have respect."

(CHAPTER EIGHT)

WHO WERE THESE PEOPLE, ANYWAY?

Jobs coughed. He could feel the grit in his mouth, on his tongue, coating his throat. He blinked against the ash in his eyes. He imagined his hair was gray with it.

Why hadn't the Marauders found more water? Jobs wondered irritably. *Where was the water?*

The bleakness of the landscape had been bearable when Jobs had known he'd be returning to the ship after an hour or so. But since the start of this macabre journey with the Marauders, Earth's oddly threatening blandness was getting to Jobs deep down.

The sun pushed through the haze of ash and provided a weak, uniform light. There was no such thing as morning, with the gradual dawning of a sunrise and its promise of a new day. There was no such thing as evening, with its slow softening of light into soothing blues and purples, and finally into the deep velvet of night.

Jobs looked up at the sky. The almost-forgotten poet in him wanted to see the stars.

A human needed variety. Mo'Steel thought he'd give anything for the sight of a ruined tree, something to vary the boring sameness of land and sky.

A cliff would be good, Mo'Steel thought. He wanted something he could jump off. He wanted something he could climb up, using tooth and nail if necessary. He wanted something he could hang from by one hand while whooping with wild delight and waving to his friends with the other hand. He wanted something he could scale or ride or conquer, but all there was as far as his eye could see was — nothing.

Mo'Steel looked at Balder, Claw, and Snipe, Newton's stupid strong-arms. Who were these people, anyway? And why did he have to play by their rules?

He almost wished for a fight right then. Almost.

Forget about my stupid leg, he vowed. *If I come across a cliff, I'm scaling it.*

Violet wiped ash from her eyes and felt like she was cracking up. She recognized the bubble of incipient hysteria rising from her gut.

It wasn't only the crude company that was driving Violet crazy. It was the lack of hope, the feeling of being at a dead end. Gray flat light, gray flat land, nothing punctuating the grayness but brief rest stops for a piece of horrid, stringy food.

Violet sighed and realized, too late, how loudly she'd sighed. She could feel eyes on her. . . . She looked to her left and saw Sanchez, trudging along, head bowed, eyes on the ground.

Was he looking at me? she wondered uneasily. *I don't want him looking at me.* She still wasn't sure if his warning had been a favor or —

Violet came to a halt and let Sanchez walk on ahead. For some reason she couldn't name, she thought then of Billy, alone out there in the gray.

Oh, Billy, she thought, *where are you?*

The band stopped briefly to eat and for Newton to inventory the food supply, something he announced loudly that he would be doing. Noyze wondered if he really suspected someone had been pilfering or if he was doing the inventory to make Mo'Steel feel inadequate. Mo'Steel was supposed to be in charge but it didn't always play out that way.

Noyze put Newton out of her mind and settled down beside Badger. He was maybe Mo'Steel's age.

Something about him reminded Noyze of Mo'Steel, though she couldn't yet say exactly what it was.

"Tell me about Yorka," she asked boldly.

Badger answered promptly, "Yorka, she was born with the Alphas."

"What's she doing with you guys?" Noyze asked.

Badger shrugged. "What j'ou think? Look at her. She can't talk. She's defective, what Alphas call a mutant, like the rest of the Marauders. The Alphas didn't want her once they found out."

Noyze was stunned. "Not even her mother?"

"Alphas are different," Badger said enigmatically.

"But maybe the reason Yorka can't talk is emotional," Noyze argued. "You know. Maybe she could have been taught to talk. She can hear, right?"

Again, Badger shrugged. "I know nothing 'bout that, an emotional reason. I know Yorka hears okay. She listens. I see it on her face, in her eyes."

Noyze wasn't about to let it go. "There are plenty of other ways to communicate without spoken words," she said. "Just because Yorka can't talk doesn't make her worthless to her community."

Badger smiled, but not happily. "J'ou tell the Alphas," he said. "Far as they concerned, j'ou not perfect, j'ou dumped with Marauders."

Noyze thought about this and shivered. So, if she

had been born after the Rock to the Alpha survivors, she, too, would have been tossed away like so
much trash. She, too, would have been stuck with a
band of wild and dirty and violent Marauders.

Still . . .

Noyze wondered as she picked at her meager,
tasteless meal. Was it really so great to spend all
your time underground, cultivating depleted soil,
performing endless boring experiments, doing soil
toxicity calculations and making ugly clothing from
tough plant fibers?

Maybe in the long run Yorka was better off with
the Marauders.

Noyze turned to Badger and took a chance.
After the hallucination of the handless man she
was more hesitant than ever to reveal a weakness
but . . .

"I was born deaf," she said. "I could hear hardly
anything until I had an operation." At Badger's puzzled look, Noyze added, "Um, when people fixed it
so I could hear."

"J'our people keep j'ou?" Badger asked, voice
hushed with amazement.

"Yup."

"Like Marauders, then. Like us," Badger said, and
Noyze thought she heard pride in his tone.

Noyze never thought she'd say it but she said it now.

"Yeah. Like you."

Badger began to smile a broken-tooth smile — and then his eyes darted over her shoulder.

"I have to go," he mumbled, and climbed to his feet.

Puzzled, Noyze watched Badger go — and saw what had scared him away.

Balder, Claw, and Snipe. Newton's posse.

Newton's big-deal inventory was taking a long time. But Olga didn't mind. She'd slept and when she woke, the pain in her head had eased. A little.

After a while, Noyze had joined her. She'd told Olga about Yorka.

When Noyze had moved off to talk to Mo'Steel, Olga had eased herself to her feet and sought out Yorka. The girl had confirmed Noyze's story. Yes, Yorka nodded, she'd been born with the Alphas. Yes, when she was little she'd been given to the Marauders. No, she didn't remember much about life underground. No, she did not know her mother.

Olga thought about her earlier conversation with Violet.

If the Alphas refused to allow those with genetic

"defects" to live as a part of their colony, what place would there ever be for Violet and Edward and D-Caf and 2Face and Roger Dodger?

What place would there be for her own son, with his replacement body parts?

Noyze's information about the Alphas' genetic policies had put a whole new spin on things. *The Marauders aren't without glaring faults*, Olga thought, *but at least you're welcome to stay if you can keep up with the pack.*

But if you were sick . . . Olga winced against a jolt of pain. When her eyes refocused, she saw Aga watching her closely.

Before Olga could react, Aga turned away.

They were on the move again. Noyze wanted to walk next to Mo'Steel but he was hedged in by men. Big, hairy, smelly men. Noyze sighed and looked around for Badger.

She spotted him and made her way to his side. He acknowledged her with a nod.

"Who gives you your names?" Noyze asked abruptly.

Badger shrugged. "Our mothers. Sometimes we change our names when we grow up. Like Claw, he used to be Bender."

"That's like us, mostly. Not like the Alphas, though. The guy named Mattock said they had a Namer to assign a name to a baby."

"Why?"

"I don't know. He didn't say. Anyway, it can't be that tough a job. A baby's only born when someone dies."

"Hawk, he killed Woody," Badger said.

"Huh. Right. I wonder if that means another girl besides Echo has been chosen to give her DNA for a baby."

Badger shook his head and shrugged.

Noyze wondered. It didn't seem likely she'd ever have a baby of her own. Not that she wanted a baby! Not now, anyway. Suddenly, Noyze felt kind of embarrassed even thinking about babies.

"Um, I'm going to check with Olga," she said abruptly, and ran off before Badger could reply.

CHAPTER NINE

"THIS IS POLITICS."

Mo'Steel watched Newton order Yorka to fetch him something. He wondered, *What if I just said, Hey, sorry, 'migo, but I don't want to be here. I am just not down with marching off to get myself killed by some big ole Beast. Thanks and all, but nope.*

What then? I'd be sliced and diced before the last word had left my mouth, Mo'Steel told himself. *And then Newton and his cronies would make toast of my mother and my best friend and Noyze. . . .*

Mo'Steel's power over the Marauders was minimal. It was a joke.

Now Newton, dragging Grost by the arm, was stalking his way. Mo'Steel got to his feet, bounced up twice on his toes, felt the effort in his bad leg. It was healing, but not fast enough.

"Here." Newton roughly shoved Grost toward

Mo'Steel. The girl stumbled but regained her uncertain footing and looked up at Mo'Steel through a rough thatch of hair.

Mo'Steel didn't understand. What was he supposed to do now?

Newton grinned, obviously enjoying Mo'Steel's hesitation. Mo'Steel saw his buddies, Snipe, Claw, and Balder, nudge one another and snicker. Suddenly, he had an audience, both Marauder and Remnant.

"J'ou and her are together like Old Berg and Aga," Newton said. And Mo'Steel suddenly knew exactly what Newton had in mind for him and Grost. A Marauder marriage.

And that was so not happening.

"Begging your pardon, but . . ."

Begging your pardon? Mo'Steel thought wildly. *Where had that come from?* He sounded like somebody's great-great-grandfather.

"But, er, no thanks," he added quickly, making what he hoped was a friendly gesture with his hands.

Immediately, Mo'Steel sensed that his refusal of Grost had been taken as an insult. And as a sign of weakness.

"J'ou say no to me?" Newton demanded.

"Meaning no disrespect . . ." he said, once again trailing off. He could sense Jobs and the others gathered around him, watching. He could feel his mother's eyes on him. And then somebody moved.

2Face sidled up to him and whispered harshly in his ear. "Don't be an idiot," she said. "It's a challenge. If you say no, you're going to look like a wimp. Just say yes and get it over with."

"No," Mo'Steel said.

2Face grabbed his arm above the elbow and squeezed. "You're messing with us all, you moron. This is politics. This isn't about morals."

Mo'Steel wrenched away from 2Face and gave her a look he hoped showed the depth of his revulsion. "*Get away from me,*" he ordered. 2Face sneered and backed off.

But what she'd said rang true in Mo'Steel's skull. For the sake of his own hide, as well as for the lives of his friends, should he reverse his decision?

For a tiny flicker of a moment the possibility seemed within reach. Mo'Steel shoved his imagination into the future. . . .

No. There was just no way he could go through with it.

For one, there was his mom, who totally wouldn't approve, and there was Mo'Steel's own respect for femmes in general. Newton's shoving Grost in his face was wrong, end of story.

Besides, there was something — wrong — with Grost. It wasn't just the half a foot. Mo'Steel was no stranger to missing — or replaced — body parts. And it wasn't just that poor Grost wasn't for him, with her small, crossed eyes and gray, broken teeth. It was that she looked like — like maybe there was something wrong with her head, inside.

Suddenly, Mo'Steel felt overwhelmed by pity for the girl. *Maybe she can't take care of herself,* he thought. *I'm a nice guy. Maybe I should take care of her. And the best way to do that would be . . .*

Not to make her his personal slave.

"Uh," he said, "with all due respect, uh, no thanks. I mean, thanks and all but . . . No. Thanks."

That was it.

Mo'Steel saw plainly the look of disappointment on Aga's face, the looks of disrespect and even disgust on the faces of the other women. Even Grost showed a spark of feeling; she flicked one torn fingernail against her teeth as if tossing away a bad piece of seed.

And on the faces of the men — Badger and Sanchez being the exceptions — Mo'Steel saw open mockery and derision.

Great, he thought. *Just great. Another test I failed, but I just couldn't. I just couldn't.*

(CHAPTER TEN)

"YOU'RE NOT HERE TO KILL ME, ARE YOU?"

2Face didn't know why she bothered. She'd tried to help that idiot Mo'Steel handle the Grost situation but he was useless. And his stupidity was going to come back and bite them all in the butt.

2Face knew that for sure.

And, she thought, stalking over to the rough circle of stinky Marauders, *it's not even like I can stage a coup. Nesia wouldn't let me be her leader for two seconds before slaughtering me.*

2Face joined Violet and Cocker just outside the ring of Marauders gathered for sleep.

"Why is Grost sleeping outside the circle by herself?" Violet asked Cocker.

"Newton don't want Grost around him no more," Cocker said evenly.

Cocker walked away and 2Face turned furiously to Violet. "We're going to pay for this," 2Face snapped. "I told him we're all going to pay for his Dudley Do-Right act."

"Mo'Steel did the only thing he could do," Violet said. She sounded weary.

2Face grunted, walked off, and threw herself down just behind Curia.

"J'ou go away," Curia hissed, turning to 2Face. "This place for us."

"What!" 2Face demanded. "We all sleep close together. It's for protection. Since when —"

"Go!"

2Face knew defeat when she met it. Angrily she got up and walked back to Violet.

"You see what's happening? They're snubbing us. They're saying, Hey, you Remnants are a bunch of weenies and —"

"It's a clash of cultures," Violet said. "It's not about courage."

"Whatever," 2Face snapped. "The point is Mo'Steel insulted them by not taking Grost."

"We'll handle the consequences," Violet said. "What's done is done."

Violet knelt and began to spread out her sleeping things. "Let's just lie down here, okay?"

2Face laughed. "You won't be so calm when someone's stuck a knife in your back."

Violet looked up at 2Face with something odd in her eyes. 2Face felt wiggly inside.

"What?" she said.

"Nothing," Violet replied, settling down on her makeshift bed. "Just that I don't think I'll be the one with the knife in my back."

It was no use. He couldn't sleep. Not with worrying about his mom and Grost and . . .

Mo'Steel struggled to his feet and winced. The throbbing in his bad leg was always most violent when he stood after being horizontal for a while.

Can I really do this? he asked himself. *No, I can't.*

The answer came swiftly and despair flooded Mo'Steel's brain. He wasn't a guy used to feeling despair. It shocked and frightened him.

It's just the leg, he told himself. *Walk around a bit, get the blood flowing normally. Once the pain dies down you'll feel fine.*

Mo'Steel limped around the sleeping bodies close to him and headed for more open turf where he was less likely to step on anyone. Where it was less likely that anyone would hear him suck in his breath in agony.

Mo'Steel pulled his tunic closer around him and tried to calm his brain. He reached for his usual easygoing nature, for his native confidence and found —

"J'ou don't go too far."

Mo'Steel whirled around on his good leg. His heart was beating madly. His nerve endings screamed.

It was Badger.

"J'ou in pain, so j'ou don't go too far," Badger said, pointing to Mo'Steel's bad leg.

"I'm okay," Mo'Steel said, hoping his voice sounded strong. "I'm fine."

Badger looked steadily at him. *He's about my age,* Mo'Steel thought. Ash-coated hair, wildly matted. Ratty clothes. But something about his face . . . Mo'Steel tried to read the guy's intent in following him — and found something interesting.

"You're not here to kill me, are you?"

Badger looked surprised for about half a second, then grinned.

"I don't kill anybody," he said. "But sometimes, I think somebody going to kill me."

Mo'Steel shifted to keep the blood flowing in his leg and said, "Why?"

Badger shrugged. "J'ou see what I see. Some Marauders . . . they different from others."

"So," Mo'Steel said, grinning now, "are you here to protect me?"

"J'ou need protection?" Badger challenged.

Mo'Steel considered before answering. "I don't know," he said finally.

Badger nodded. "J'ou let me know when you decide."

Mo'Steel watched as Badger walked back toward the sleeping camp.

Huh, he thought. *I think I just found me an ally.*

Violet had slept well but not long. She couldn't get 2Face's words out of her mind. In spite of the calm exterior she'd shown 2Face, she was worried that Mo'Steel's rejection of Grost would backfire on them. She didn't really think there was anything she could do to prevent something bad from happening, but . . .

Violet looked for Sanchez and found him sitting quietly on the outskirts of camp. For a second she hesitated to disturb him but a growing sense of worry compelled her.

"Sanchez?"

He looked up at Violet and fixed her with those dark, knowing eyes. Again Violet realized that in another time and place she would be crazy about this guy.

"Yes?" he said.

"Can you tell me more about the Beasts?"

"Yes, I can," Sanchez said. "But no, I won't."

Violet fought down a mix of annoyance and frustration. Sanchez might be intelligent and relatively good-looking but he was a pain in the butt.

"Do you mean you won't tell me now?" she said, crouching at his side. "Will you tell me later?"

Sanchez's face was carefully without expression. It made Violet more frustrated.

"I think you want us all to die," she snapped. "You want Mo'Steel to be killed by the Beasts. You want that jerk Newton to be leader!"

Sanchez waited a beat before speaking.

Finally, he said, "I want what is best for all."

Violet fought back surprising tears.

"And you think you know what's best?" she said, voice breaking. "You don't know anything about me. About us."

Sanchez looked carefully at Violet and she saw a flicker of sadness in his eyes.

"No. I don't know anything."

CHAPTER ELEVEN

"WE DON'T NEED ANY MORE TROUBLE THAN WE ALREADY HAVE."

They'd eaten and 2Face was still roaringly hungry. Which, of course, was Billy's fault.

As was the fact that there were no books, no television, no stereo, no portable sound systems, nothing to do for recreation. Except watch the Marauder pigs go about their disgusting business.

Like the big pig Snipe. 2Face watched as Snipe dug into the skin pouch and came out with about a dozen grayish pellets. She watched as Claw grabbed the pouch and did the same, then passed the pouch to Balder.

"What is that stuff?" she whispered. "It looks like droppings of some sort."

"Droppings?" D-Caf repeated.

"You're a regular rocket scientist, aren't you?" 2Face spat. "Droppings. Excrement. Poop."

D-Caf giggled. "Poop."

"Why didn't the Alphas tell us about this?" Noyze said.

"I don't know. Maybe they were overwhelmed by our sudden appearance." Jobs paused and ran his hand over his eyes. "I mean, I would have been. Maybe they're scared of the Marauders."

"Definitely scared," Olga agreed.

2Face frowned. "Well, bully for the Alphas. But I say we don't eat any of these — poops. Even if they're harmless to Newton and his gang, who knows what they might do to us? The Marauders might have built up a resistance to any bad side effects. Our bodies might just — explode."

And I bet that's exactly what they want, 2Face thought grimly. *To poison us all and watch our guts come screaming out through our skin.*

"Right. Didn't your mother ever warn you not to take candy from strangers?" Olga said.

"Frankly, no," Violet said. "My mother was too busy building a corporate empire to worry about her daughter's well-being. But I figured it out on my own."

2Face scanned their small group, all there but for Mo'Steel. "Everybody gets it, right? Edward, Roger Dodger? You, D-Caf? Nobody touches the stuff. We don't need any more trouble than we already have."

Edward nodded solemnly. Roger Dodger checked Edward's reaction and then nodded, too. D-Caf looked grumpy with resentment at being lumped with the two younger kids but shrugged his agreement. At least, 2Face thought the shrug meant agreement. She didn't really care so much if the twitch got himself exploded.

Olga felt the pain descending again. Before it hit full force there was something she had to do. 2Face's talk of the Marauders retaliating for Mo'Steel's refusal of Newton's loathsome offer had made her think.

Olga made her way through the quieting camp to where Aga was repairing a tear in a tunic. She sat hunched over the work, squinting, using a small blunt instrument to puncture the material.

"Here," Olga said, bending down, "let me give you the needle the Alphas gave me. It's for all of us."

She reached under her tunic and felt for her shirt pocket. Aga tossed the torn tunic behind her and stood.

"I don't need no help from j'ou," she said, eyes darting to right and left.

Olga held out the needle.

"Oh, but . . ."

"No," Aga repeated. "Marauders do things our own way."

In spite of her strong words, Olga saw Aga's eyes flick with envy to the sharp needle. The needle would make her work easier. Aga knew that. Of course she wanted the needle. But . . .

"Can you tell me why what my son did was wrong?" Olga blurted. "Don't you see by refusing to be Grost's — master — he was showing his respect for her? It doesn't mean he won't protect her."

Aga opened her mouth, then snapped it shut. Olga wondered. Either she really didn't know what to say or didn't want to say what was really on her mind.

"I thought we were — friends," Olga said.

Again, Aga said nothing but her face spoke volumes. On it Olga read a struggle between extremes. Fearful hate of a stranger warred with sympathy for another woman.

Olga took one more chance.

"My son is a good person," she said. "The more he learns of the Marauders' ways the better he can fight. The better he can lead. I wish you would trust me."

Aga laughed a small, bitter laugh.

"It's not j'ou I don't trust," she said.

Olga wanted to know more but Aga turned abruptly and walked away. Olga sighed, then spotted Aga's pack. Carefully she threaded the needle through the flap and went off to sleep.

"Olga! Wake up!"

Olga sat up fast and felt the world of her dreams spin away. And her head pound.

"What?" she gasped.

2Face grabbed her arm and helped her rise.

"It's that idiot D-Caf. I think he took some of those pellets. He's having a fit or something."

Olga stumbled over to where several people were crouched. She could barely make out a pair of shoeless feet, twitching on the ground.

"Why did he do it?" Violet cried. "We told him not to take any of the pellets!"

"Oh, jeez, he's a mess!" Roger Dodger said fretfully.

"Is he going to die?" Edward asked fearfully.

"He'll be okay," Jobs answered weakly.

Olga pushed through the sick headache. She had to help the kid. The stupid kid.

"Let me through," she said. "Jobs, you keep the Marauders away. Take Edward and Roger Dodger with you."

Jobs looked afraid but moved off with the two younger boys.

Olga knelt next to Violet. Suddenly, D-Caf's body convulsed like a huge wave, then slammed straight to the ground, then his limbs began to twitch madly and Olga couldn't help but remember what Yago used to call D-Caf: the little twitch.

"Violet, you're going to have to grab hold of his tongue." Olga fumbled in her pockets and came up with a twig left over from their last meal and thrust it at Violet. "We can't let him swallow it."

Violet did as she was told, wordlessly. *A good assistant,* Olga thought. *Which makes me the doctor. And I have no idea what to do now.*

"Romeo!" she called. Mo'Steel appeared with a skid on the ash.

"What can I do, Mom?" he said. "God —"

D-Caf's body thrashed wildly again. Violet lost her grip on his tongue, cursed, grabbed for it again.

"Help me hold him down," Olga panted, crawling to reach D-Caf's arms, now behind his head. "He's going to hurt himself."

Mo'Steel grabbed D-Caf's legs and held them firmly. Vaguely, Olga was aware of voices, questioning, laughing, curious.

"2Face!" she called. "2Face!"

The girl had kept away but now she approached.

"I knew he'd do something stupid," she said angrily.

"Look," Olga instructed, "go talk to Aga. Tell her what we think happened. Tell her what's happening! See if she has anything that might help. Go!"

D-Caf began to moan and 2Face turned away with a look of disgust. "I'm going," she said.

Olga's headache was growing, fed by the horror of the situation. *Please,* she prayed, *God, let him be okay and let me be okay and . . .*

2Face was back, with Aga. The Marauder woman said nothing but nodded at Olga. Olga sighed with relief; she'd been afraid Aga would deny help.

Aga pushed Violet aside, lifted D-Caf's head, and managed to spill a tiny amount of a liquid down his throat. Olga watched as Aga turned D-Caf's head to face the ground — Olga let go of D-Caf's hands — and almost immediately, the kid vomited.

Olga fought the gorge rising in her own throat and fell back. Violet stood abruptly but Mo'Steel still held D-Caf's feet.

The vomiting was over just as suddenly as it had come and Aga laid D-Caf back down on the ground.

"He'll be good now," she said, rising.

"Thank you, thank you," Olga gasped.

Aga nodded and walked off.

2Face leaned in close to D-Caf's face. "Hey, Freak Show, you okay?"

"I don't think he'll be able to hear you for a while," Olga said, lying back on the ground.

"It was Balder that did it."

Olga sat up again. It was Badger. Noyze stood next to him.

"What?" 2Face said.

"Balder forced it on him, made him swallow. I saw it."

"Why didn't you try to stop him?" 2Face demanded, getting to her feet.

"Easy," Olga murmured.

Badger laughed uneasily. "Balder? He'd kill me."

"It's okay, Badger," Olga said as forcefully as she could manage with the nausea rising again. "It's okay. Someone . . . cover him up. I'll . . . I'll stay with him, right here. . . ."

Olga closed her eyes. As she lay back on the ground, fighting not to vomit, she thought, *Aga. Balder. One good. One bad. What claim do we have on the Marauders, anyway? Why should a hardened, experienced band of nomads be responsible for the lives of us troublesome newbies?*

Before her brain could answer those questions, Olga passed out.

The camp was astir. There was a huge uneasiness in the air. And there was laughter. The mean, nasty kind, and it was coming from Newton and his buddies.

Mo'Steel's jaw tightened as he packed up to move on.

He was not about to let the incident go. A Marauder had made a direct attack on a Remnant — and it was his fault. 2Face was right. By refusing to make Grost his personal slave, Mo'Steel had further alienated the Marauders. Maybe that had been a mistake. But he wouldn't make another one. He'd show everyone who was boss.

Question was — how? Mo'Steel glanced around camp. He knew he couldn't pit his friends against the Marauders in a flat-out fight. No way would Jobs and all the rest come out alive. And he wasn't sure of how many Marauders he could count on to pledge him their allegiance. Maybe none.

And, Mo'Steel thought, *I don't want to endanger what might be the one chance we have of making a decent life in this godforsaken place by getting myself killed before we reach the Beasts. 'Cause if for some reason I do manage to kill a Beast, then I'm officially in as leader and maybe, just maybe, Mom and Noyze and everyone else can live with the Alphas in their sort-of-decent bunker.*

Mo'Steel flexed his bad leg. He knew he'd better come up with something soon, before Newton decided Mo'Steel was afraid of him. *Which I am,* he added silently, *but that's another story.*

Controlling the limp as best he could, Mo'Steel made his way over to Newton and his cronies. As he approached, the men fell silent. Mo'Steel realized that except for the wail of one of the children, everyone in the camp had gone silent.

Balder, Claw, and Snipe shoved one another, nodded at Mo'Steel, and grinned wildly.

Mo'Steel stopped about ten feet from Newton, who had moved in front of his posse. For a moment they stared at each other without speaking. Mo'Steel was acutely aware of his physical disadvantage.

The words came out without plan.

"I want you to let Grost sleep within the circle."

"That's not how —" Newton began.

"I don't care," Mo'Steel shot back. "We do this my way. She's in the circle."

Newton shrugged elaborately.

Mo'Steel half turned away, then turned back, as if a thought had just occurred to him.

"Oh, and Newton," he said, laying his hand on his knife. "If there's another attack on my people . . ."

Newton grinned. "No attack. An accident."

"If there's one more attack," Mo'Steel repeated, "you'll pay."

"Me? I didn't do nothing," Newton said, a grin breaking across his cruddy face.

Mo'Steel urged his eyes to bore a hole in the jerk's skull.

"Yeah," he said, "maybe not. Maybe you're all Mr. Innocent. But I seriously doubt it. So if anything else happens, you — and only you — are going to pay. You get me?"

Newton's grin faded. Mo'Steel stalked off before the Marauder could reply.

Well, he thought, *I wonder if I scared him.*

Something told him he hadn't.

CHAPTER TWELVE

"J'OU GOT SOMETHING WE CAN USE?"

They'd be on their way again soon. Jobs was ready to go. He stood off by himself, watching Edward impress his new friends by blending into each one in turn.

Jobs hadn't even thought to warn Edward not to go chameleon in front of the Marauders. Should he have? Now Edward was clearly over whatever shyness it was that had prevented the mutation from occurring before.

"Can't he stop doing that?" Violet demanded, suddenly at his side.

"No, I don't think he can." Jobs spoke calmly, but inside he felt anything but calm. He and Violet had hardly spoken since she'd revealed her own mutation. It hadn't been his choice. "It's not like — uh, it's not like, you know, Tate's thing —"

"Go ahead and say it," Violet spit out. "Or my 'thing.' It's a mutation, Jobs. Me, 2Face, Roger

Dodger, D-Caf, Edward — we're a freak show. A traveling freak show. And I'm not sure how wise it is for the Marauders to know about — us."

"They won't know about you and the others if you — if you control it."

"Great," Violet muttered. "Look who's coming."

Jobs turned away from the kids. It was Newton, striding toward them.

Newton came up to Jobs and Violet. His eyes were intense.

"How does he do that?" he said, nodding toward Edward.

"We don't know," Violet said quickly. "He just can. It's no big deal."

They watched as Edward shimmered into sight, then receded once more into the bland, bleak landscape.

Newton laughed. "It's a big deal. Maybe he teach us all how to —"

"Blend in," Jobs said automatically. "Like a chameleon."

"What j'ou say?" Newton said suspiciously.

Jobs cringed. The last thing he wanted was for Newton to think he was trying to pull something over on him. Or that he was mocking Newton's limited knowledge.

"Oh, right," he said. "A chameleon. It's an animal from Before. It changed its color to blend into the environment. For camouflage. Protection against enemies."

Okay, Jobs thought as a sly grin came to Newton's face. Enemies were something Newton knew all about.

"Yeah, protection against enemies, like them Beasts. I watch the kid, I see what I see." Suddenly, Newton turned to them with sharp eyes.

"J'ou got anything like that going on?" he demanded. "J'ou got something we can use?"

"No," Jobs said flatly.

Violet shook her head and said nothing.

Newton continued to eye them with suspicion. "We see," he said, then abruptly walked off.

"He didn't believe us," Violet said, her voice betraying an edge of panic.

"He can't make you — us — do anything," Jobs said fiercely, as if to convince himself. "Mo'Steel warned him about hurting us. Newton can't make you — do it."

"Maybe not me," Violet admitted. "But if he makes 2Face angry enough? Or D-Caf — he's a loose cannon. And since Balder tried to poison him he's twitchier than ever. Roger Dodger's just a kid —"

"Don't worry about it," Jobs snapped.

"You really think Newton is afraid of Mo'Steel?" Violet pressed. "I don't. I think he thinks Mo'Steel's bluffing. I —"

"Just stop talking about it!" Jobs shouted.

Violet gave him an odd, appraising look and turned away.

The end of the "day's" journey. The band was gathered for a meal. Violet eyed her portion of food warily, searching for any tidbit that looked tasty. *What I wouldn't do for a big, juicy apple,* she thought.

Violet pushed away the fantasies of good food and got down to the unappetizing business of eating. *I need my strength,* she told herself. *I don't want to starve to death. Starvation is slow and painful. Keep that in mind.*

"Have you heard anything specific about the Beasts?" Olga whispered. "I've been trying to learn something concrete and, well, believable, but I've got nothing so far. I think the Marauders are withholding information to frighten us."

"I tried to find out something from Sanchez," Violet answered, grateful for the interruption. "But he wouldn't tell me anything. Besides, he's a storyteller, not a researcher of facts. He's like the wise man."

"Isn't he sort of young for the role?" Olga said.

Violet nodded. "Yes. Sanchez told me he was being apprenticed by a guy named Rexer. Rexer died a while back, though, taking lots of tales with him, stories everybody else sort of knows but not in the way Rexer did."

"Huh. Memory being as faulty and as creative and as individual as it is, who knows the real truth about the Beasts?"

"We will," Violet said grimly. "When we find them."

Suddenly, Sanchez began to speak and everyone fell silent.

"Soon," he began, "soon it will be time for Marauders and Alphas alike to travel to the Source."

Violet noted the ripple of surprise and excitement that ran through the Marauder band. Sanchez paused just long enough to let it die down and then resumed speaking.

"This journey," he went on, "has not been taken for a long, long time, since before the living memory of Rexer. But before he died, Rexer, in his wisdom, taught me how to see some things. And now, I see that soon, very soon, the Marauders must make the journey. We must go to the Source."

"But why?" Cocker said, his tone awestruck.

Sanchez nodded. "The why, that I have not yet seen. Maybe the why will come clear before it is time to go, maybe not. What I know, I will tell."

Violet and Olga shared a look of intense curiosity. But Mo'Steel spoke before they could.

"What's the Source?" he said bluntly.

"It a private thing, to Marauders only," Rattler snapped.

"And Alphas," Sanchez corrected. "And yes, even to the Savagers. The Source belongs to all of those who live Now."

"Like us," Mo'Steel said, his voice controlled. "Like every one of us."

No one responded.

Violet couldn't keep silent any longer. "If the Source is so secret and special," she asked, "why did you mention it in front of us? Like it or not, Mo'Steel's your acting leader. Our acting leader. Doesn't he have a right to know everything?"

"Not everything," Sanchez declared, fingering the piece of metal he wore around his neck. "Not everything." He sighed and, after another moment, spoke again.

"This much I will tell j'ou. More will be told when — if — a certain thing comes to pass. The Source is ancient. The Source is a place of great power. There lies a sacred object, the one sacred object of the people. It is said that from the Source we come and that to the Source we must return when She calls to us. She calls to us now. And soon, very soon, we will go to Her. But first, a certain thing must come to pass."

"Well, that's helpful," Olga whispered dryly.

"Okay," Mo'Steel said. "Fair enough."

Violet silently applauded his sense of when to let go. *Mo'Steel does make a good leader,* she thought. *He's smart. And he's incorruptible.*

Violet was startled out of her thoughts by a gruff voice.

"What j'ou have to say?" Claw challenged now. "J'ou people have story to tell? We want to hear a good story."

Violet felt all eyes turn to her. *Why me?* she thought. Then: *If not me, then who?*

She knew it had better be a story the Marauders would really like. So, she decided, it probably should have a lot of action. Okay. Maybe some romance?

But what do Marauder women know of romance? Violet thought, shooting a glance at Nesia and Curia. They'd probably think that Romeo was a wimp. They'd probably jeer Prince Charming off the stage.

Violet thought of Heathcliff from *Wuthering Heights,* the wild and angry hero, but then realized she didn't remember enough of the book to tell a good tale.

Dr. Jekyll and Mr. Hyde? Too incendiary. *Around the World in Eighty Days?* No. Violet's mind began to blank. *Come on, come on,* she told herself, *think.* Sanchez was looking at her steadily, his face devoid of expression. *A good actor,* Violet thought. *I bet that inside he's roaring with laughter.*

"Ideas?" she hissed.

"Don't underestimate the audience," Noyze advised. "Everyone's got an imagination. Challenge them."

"I don't want to give them any bad ideas."

"People get bad ideas whether you give them to them or not," Noyze said impatiently. "Come on!"

"Okay. Okay." Violet cleared her throat and began. "This is a very old story called 'Jack and the Beanstalk.'"

There was a murmur of curiosity from the Marauders. *So far, so good,* Violet thought and plunged on with the tale. As she spoke she called up every ounce of dramatic energy she possessed: She used her hands, eyes, and voice to express emotion; when she got to the part where the giant chased Jack to the top of the beanstalk, Violet got to her feet and pounded and roared. She made the giant's final, deadly fall as grotesque and as bloody as she could. She made Jack as clever as he ever was told and his mother as angry one moment as she was elated the next.

"And Jack and his mother lived happily ever after," she said finally, suddenly embarrassed to be standing and the center of rapt attention.

"Nice job," Mo'Steel whispered.

Violet dropped to the ground. And then it happened.

Aga led the Marauders in a burst of rhythmic hooting and foot stomping and all but little Tackie joined in enthusiastically.

When the frenzy had died down, Sanchez spoke. "That was very good," he said, and Violet blushed as he smiled.

"I liked that giant smashing his head!" That was Balder. "I could kill a giant!"

"Yeah, that Jack, he something!" Cocker enthused.

"J'ou'll tell us another story?" Sanchez asked.

Flush with success, Violet nodded. "Okay," she said, taking a deep breath. "This is a story called 'Little Red Riding Hood.'"

"Good one," Jobs murmured. "Don't forget the part about the woodsman cutting open the wolf's stomach at the end."

Violet glanced quickly at him and smiled. "Thanks," she said. "I won't."

CHAPTER THIRTEEN

"I JUST WISH HE HADN'T HAD TO GO ALONE."

Jobs knelt in the ash and listlessly tied his pack closed. It would be his pillow. Mo'Steel crouched by him, his gaze wandering around the group.

"Leg okay?" Jobs asked.

"Hmm? Oh, yeah, it's getting there." Mo'Steel made a goofy face. "Hey, I'm Mo'Majesty, I'm invincible."

Jobs tried to work up a smile but it didn't come. "I can't help but wonder what happened to Billy," he said instead. "Do you think the Alphas found him?"

Mo'Steel shrugged. "Even if they did, would they take him in? Let's face it, Billy is seriously odd, definitely not a normal human specimen. It might be better for him if the Alphas don't find him."

Jobs didn't like to hear that, but couldn't totally dismiss the truth in his friend's words.

"I don't know," he said after a moment. "He's

probably dead by now. If the storm didn't make him kill himself, then a pillar of flame could have gotten him. Or the Beasts. Or — I don't know what."

"Starvation," Mo'Steel suggested. "Dehydration."

"I feel bad," Jobs said, aware that his voice was rising with every word. "I feel we should have formed a search party to look for him. Before we headed out with the Marauders."

Mo'Steel shook his head. "Come on, Duck. You heard what that Alpha woman named Westie said just before we left. She said it was sure Billy was already —"

"I know, I know," Jobs said, his voice ragged. "But still. I always liked Billy, right from the beginning, way back at Cape Canaveral. I always respected him. And I always felt bad for him, I guess. I just wish he . . . I just wish he hadn't had to die alone."

Mo'Steel shrugged again. "Not much we can do about that now. I'm sorry, too, but —"

Newton shouted for Mo'Steel.

Mo'Steel rolled his eyes. "I gotta go. Duty and all. You going to be okay?" he asked.

Jobs set his lips tightly and nodded.

Watching Mo'Steel lope off, Jobs suddenly knew the truth. It came to him in a flash. How could he have been so blind?

Mo'Steel had wanted Billy gone.

They all had wanted Billy gone. No one cared about Billy but him. No one ever had, except Big Bill, but he was long gone so it was all about Jobs now. Jobs had cared and he still did. Everybody was against Billy and because he, Jobs, cared about Billy that meant that everyone was against him, too. It was logical, wasn't it, that if you hated or feared someone, by extension you hated or feared his friends.

Watch your back, Jobs, he told himself. *Trust no one. Not even your best friend. The guy you thought was your best friend.*

Jobs put his fingers to his temples. The pressure inside his skull was building.

Billy reached down inside himself, felt the relentless fluttering of his heart, and squeezed the life out of it.

He squeezed, then he squeezed harder.

Ah, yes. The synapses of his brain, firing alone, all alone.

Then, peace. Stillness. Quiet.

He was alone. Alone at last, the last thing he'd ever thought he'd want again. Alone — and dead.

I am dead, aren't I? Billy thought, and then knew.

No, I'm not dead. I'm thinking. You don't have thoughts if you're dead.

How would you know? he asked himself. *You've never been dead before.*

You don't ask questions if you're dead. If you're dead you have all the answers.

I . . .

Billy's eyes flew open. He saw gray, gray, he was in some sort of semi-enclosed space and it was gray.

But that voice, that last one, it . . .

Who . . . ?

You can't die, Billy. Please, don't die.

I . . .

We can't let you die, Billy, we're sorry. You see, you're our manifestation.

I'm your . . .

Right, we're alive, Billy, but only because you're alive, so don't go dying, okay, kid?

If I die, you die?

That's what we're thinking. Unless, of course, first you get us downloaded in some other head or machine or maybe on some disk—hell, we don't know. We're all smart, that's why we were on the Mayflower in the first place, but this stuff, what's happened to us? Hey, this was sci-fi back home.

There is no home, Billy said.

Silence.

Who are you? How come I never saw you before? Billy said. *How come you never talked to me before?*

The first voice again. *We are who you called the Missing Five, Billy.*

Billy closed his eyes again. He was tired. He'd wanted to die, he'd tried to die. Maybe that was why these five didn't seem in the least familiar.

Maybe if he knew their names.

Who . . . who are you? he asked. *I mean, who were you Before?*

Does it matter now, Billy?

Yes, Billy said. *It does.*

There were other people in his head.

It mattered.

Get up, Billy. Go to the Source.

The Source?

We will guide you. Go now. The Time is approaching.

Why won't you tell me who you are?

In time, Billy. In time.

(CHAPTER FOURTEEN)

"SHE SAYS NO ONE HAS EVER GOTTEN OUT ALIVE."

Violet became aware of a darkening ahead. It was subtle, a gradual deepening of shade. Violet wasn't even sure it was real. She was so eager for change she might easily have been imagining it.

She hung back to wait for Olga.

"Do you see it?" Violet asked.

Olga squinted ahead. "If you mean the dark, yeah, I see it."

Violet sighed. "Good. I thought I was imagining it."

"I wish you had been," Olga said, and her voice was tight. "If it's the Dark Zone, my son is running out of time. We all are."

Violet was surprised. "I thought you had confidence in Mo'Steel."

"I do. What I don't have is trust in the Marauders. At least not in Newton and his gang. They're going to pull something, I know it."

"What if we don't let them?" Violet said, aware that she was being ridiculous. "Or, I don't know, what if Aga and Cocker and Badger stick up for us? For Mo'Steel."

Olga didn't respond right away. When she did, she said, "The Beasts. Aga told me she thinks Newton's been lying about having killed a Beast. She says no one has ever gotten out alive. What chance does that leave Mo'Steel?"

Violet looked ahead to the darkness.

She had no answer for Olga.

The band stopped to eat and rest about two miles from the big spooky dark place. The Dark Zone. Jeez.

"I'm cold," D-Caf said.

"What do you want me to do about it?" 2Face snapped.

The twitch shrugged.

"Look, we're all miserable, all right? And it's only going to get colder once we're actually in the Dark Zone. So deal with it. Don't let these animals see any more weakness than you can help, okay?"

D-Caf hung his head. 2Face sighed and turned her back on him.

Newton was talking with Mo'Steel. 2Face wondered what they said to each other when they were alone like that. Probably: "J'ou will die." Then: "No, you will."

Macho idiots, all of them.

The two parted and Mo'Steel signaled for Jobs while Newton signaled for Cocker. 2Face continued to watch as the guys set about building a fire. The Marauders had come prepared. Cocker opened one of the packs he carried and took out two compact bundles of — paper? Plant fiber, 2Face guessed, something maybe the Alphas had given them to work with, or something the Marauders had just taken. Maybe the bundles were made of something found in the ashy ruins of Before. . . . *What's he going to light them with?* 2Face wondered.

"The fire is for more than warmth."

2Face startled. Badger had snuck up on her.

"Don't do that, okay?" she said testily.

Badger looked blank.

2Face rolled her eyes. "The fire. What else is it for?"

"To keep away the enemies. From now on, we'll carry fire as we walk."

"Like, torches?" 2Face said warily. *As long as I*

don't have to carry one, she added silently, touching the destroyed skin of her face. They were bound to be heavy — and dangerous.

Badger nodded. "Remember, j'ou stick close to a torch, don't wander away."

"I'll remember," 2Face said. "Don't worry about me."

The band was gathered around the fire. Mo'Steel was a basic enough guy to admit that it was kind of nice, kind of like camping.

Except no marshmallows. And the fact that in the past hours everyone, even the kids, had grown quieter and the mood more tense.

"Now is the time," Newton announced suddenly.

Mo'Steel wondered if Newton realized how pompous he sounded and figured the Marauder knew exactly.

"Okay," Mo'Steel replied casually.

Newton frowned. "J'ou want to know what it is time for?"

Mo'Steel wasn't a big fan of mind games; he was a guy of action. Still, it was fun to goof on Newton.

"Yeah," he said with a shrug, "sure, whatever."

Newton's frown became a grimace and Mo'Steel decided he'd pretend to pay the guy some respect. "I mean, tell me what it's time for. I want — I need — to know."

Newton didn't stop frowning but at least he didn't swing a punch. For that, Mo'Steel was glad.

"It is time for j'ou to know about the Beasts," Newton announced. "Time for j'ou to get ready for the big battle. The battle that will decide."

Mo'Steel nodded, hoping for a nonchalant air, but inside, his guts had begun to boil.

"The Beasts," Newton intoned, "have fur all over their bodies, except for their hands and feet. These are covered in tough skin, very wrinkled skin. Out of this skin come very thick, very sharp claws. The Beasts have long tails, like whips, very dangerous. The Beasts have long, very thin needles sticking out from their faces. Some say these have poison. Their faces are long and pointed. Their teeth are very sharp, like knives. Some say poison lies in the bite of the Beasts, not in the prick of the needles."

Mo'Steel said silently, *Note to self: Avoid entire face area.*

"The Beasts fight in a swarm," Newton went on, voice lowering, "most times. They trample j'ou. But

103

here's what j'ou gotta do. J'ou gotta cut away the leader, get him alone. When j'ou do, the others, they back off and now it's just j'ou and him."

"But first I have to get him alone," Mo'Steel repeated.

"Yeah." Newton grinned malevolently. "No one but I ever done that and live to tell the story."

Mo'Steel caught flickers of doubt and amusement on the faces of some of the Marauders. It seemed that not everyone bought Newton's self-aggrandizing tale.

"Tell us more about the Beasts."

That was Violet. She shot Mo'Steel a look he couldn't quite read and looked back at Newton.

Mo'Steel caught Newton's smug, pleased expression and silently thanked Violet for her question.

"Once every while the Beasts hold a council and decide what they do. They decide to keep the leader or they decide it is time for him to go. If it is time for him to go, the leader agrees to be killed. His body is used in a ceremony to honor Beast ancestors. No Marauder ever see this ceremony, but we hear."

From whom? Mo'Steel wondered. *Do the Beasts have double agents running around?*

"The new leader," Newton went on, "is chosen

by election. But the new leader must prove worthy by accepting the challenge of the Beast Leveler."

"Who's that?" Violet asked.

Newton nodded at Sanchez.

"In the Beast band," Sanchez explained, "there are some who are head warriors. The strongest of these is known as the Beast Leveler. It is his role to challenge the new leader. It is a fight to the end. If the Beast Leveler wins, the council chooses another as a new leader and now this new leader must fight the Beast Leveler."

"Poor Leveler," D-Caf said loudly. "He's got to stick around until someone kills him."

"It an honor to die for the Beast band!" Balder said forcefully.

"I find it hard to believe that guy knows anything about honor," Olga whispered.

"Maybe Balder wants to defect to the Beasts," Noyze whispered back. "He's hairy enough."

"Doesn't the strong warrior, the Leveler, ever stage a coup?" Mo'Steel asked Newton, aware of what he was implying. "Just seize power?"

Newton's eyes sank into an angry glare. It was a moment before he spoke again. When he did, Mo'Steel heard the ice in his voice.

"This never happens with the Beasts," he said. "The Beasts have rules. They have honor."

"Just like the Marauders?" Mo'Steel said, matching Newton's steely gaze and cold, calm tone.

Newton didn't reply.

"God, it sounds as if the Beasts are — sentient." Noyze paused. "Is that possible?"

Violet laughed bitterly. "You're asking about possibility? Look around. Would any of us have thought any of this possible?"

"I guess. Unless this has all been a seriously bad dream."

"Call me crazy," Violet said, "but I'm pretty sure I'm not living in a soap opera. The dead ain't coming back to life and no one's having anyone's love child."

"What's a love child?" a young voice asked.

Violet jumped. She hadn't even known Edward was listening. *Of course you didn't,* she scolded silently. *He's almost invisible!*

"Uh, nothing," she answered inanely.

"A chimpanzee, I could expect," Olga said now. "But a rat? An overgrown, mutant rat? That's just frightening."

"Rats caused the Black Death, you know," Noyze

said. "Or maybe they just spread it, something like that."

"A rat ran over my dad's shoe once," Roger Dodger said. "He told me."

"I'm sure it did," Violet said, weariness overtaking her. "And I'm sure it was a big fat rat. Now, let's try to get some sleep, okay?"

"They want to scare j'ou."

Mo'Steel opened his eyes, startled. Badger was standing over him. He looked menacing silhouetted by the fire, though Mo'Steel recognized that Badger was not a threat.

Slowly, he sat up. Badger crouched by his side.

"Well, they did a fine job, then," Mo'Steel said.

Badger cracked a smile.

"So, are the Beasts really as bad as all that? Be honest, 'migo."

"What's ''migo'?" Badger said.

"Oh. Right. It's really 'amigo.' It's Spanish for friend. Buddy."

"Spanish. That was one of the old languages. From a country called Spain. That was in a continent called Europe."

"Yeah. How did you learn about that?" Mo'Steel asked.

Badger shrugged. "I learn things from when we at the Alphas' colony. But j'ou, j'ou all come from United States of America, right? How do j'ou know Spanish?"

Mo'Steel grinned. "You really interested in a history lesson? I'm no scholar but I know enough."

Badger settled more comfortably on the ground and nodded.

"Okay, then. Lesson one. I'll tell you about what Earth was like just before the Rock hit."

Mo'Steel talked about water. He told Badger about rivers and oceans and lakes and streams. He explained about rain — as best as he could remember the science part of it — and about snow and storms, about puddles and swimming pools. He described waterfalls. He told Badger about plumbing and about expensive water in bottles. He told him about lawns and gardens and watering restrictions and droughts.

Badger listened and time passed. Finally, Mo'Steel said, "You bored yet?"

Badger grinned. "No, 'migo. Not bored. But I'm not believing all that about water! J'ou tell me more later?"

"Yeah, sure. Hey," Mo'Steel said, "tell me: Are

you the only one of your group interested in the past? I mean, the Before time, pre-Rock?"

Badger shrugged. "Don't know. Maybe not. But there's a fear about back then. About — j'ou." Badger's voice lowered. "J'ou all from the first ship, the *Mayflower*? J'ou all should be dead. But j'ou're alive. People want to know why. And how. They think maybe j'ou have some secret powers. That maybe j'ou're just some ghosts come to trick us. Maybe. Others, they think, what are j'ou doing here, messing into our lives? J'ou don't belong."

"Badger, we haven't belonged for a long, long time," Mo'Steel said sadly. "Ain't nothing new in that."

Badger got to his feet. "That's okay by me," he whispered.

Mo'Steel watched him bunk down next to Yorka.

Well, he thought as he lay back down in the semi-dark. *That was interesting.*

CHAPTER FIFTEEN

"HE CRAZY, THIS ONE."

Jobs felt jumpy. The scritching feet were haunting him, following him, then scooting out of sight the moment he whirled to find them. The growing cold was depressing him. The ghosts were watching him, their eyes sad and black.

Jobs's feet hurt. He wished he had something tougher than sneakers on his feet. Maybe hiking boots. Jobs thought of warm sun and pine trees and fresh running streams and tiny white butter-flies. . . .

He stopped and whirled around.

Nothing. Nothing but odd, questioning looks from Noyze and Badger as they passed him by.

Water, Jobs thought. *I need some water.* His tongue felt fat in his mouth.

Who had the water? Cocker was carrying a

load. *He'll give me some water,* Jobs thought, urging his weary feet to hurry and catch up with Cocker.

"Cocker!" he called.

The Marauder stopped, turned, and waited for Jobs.

"Can I . . ." Jobs breathed heavily. Why couldn't he breathe? "I . . . Can I have some of my water?"

"J'ou can wait till we rest?" Cocker asked. Jobs thought Cocker was looking at him with suspicion. Why was that?

He shook his head. "No," he croaked.

Cocker continued to look at him carefully for a long moment, then reached for a large Beast bladder.

"Open j'ours," he instructed.

Jobs fumbled with the cap of his small bladder and held it out. He noted with some surprise that his hands were trembling.

Slowly and with great care, Cocker poured the precious water into Jobs's bladder.

"J'our portion. Drink wisely," Cocker said, recapping the large bladder.

Jobs nodded and eagerly took a sip. It was grand. With his still-trembling hand he began to replace the cap on his bladder . . .

And whirled around, tripping over his own

sneaker laces, searching for the scritching feet and the sad black eyes and falling to the ground in a tangled heap, watching the water, the precious water, spill out onto the ash and disappear.

"J'ou crazy!" Cocker shouted, and dragged Jobs to his feet. He yanked the small bladder from Jobs's hand and shook it.

"Empty," he said, thrusting it back to Jobs.

Jobs wanted to cry. He'd lost his water and those tiny little feet were after him, and the ghosts, they were laughing. . . .

"What happened?" someone shouted.

It was Newton, stomping back through the band. "Keep moving!" he shouted now to some of the others who'd stopped and were staring back at Jobs.

"Stop staring at me," Jobs whispered.

Again, Cocker eyed him funny.

Newton reached them and Cocker said, "He crazy, this one. He asked for his water. He look sick so I give it to him. Then — he falls down and the water all spilled. Not one drop left."

The trembling began to move up Jobs's arms now and into his chest. His heart was fluttering madly.

Newton gestured for Cocker to go on. Jobs saw him hesitate. Newton growled and Cocker walked away.

"I didn't . . ." Jobs began. "I'm sorry."

What else can I say? Jobs thought, panic racing through his blood. *He's going to kill me. He's just going to kill me. Then the ghosts will be happy. Their eyes will be bright. Then the feet will stop following me.*

The big Marauder's eyes blazed. He loomed over Jobs like a monster out of a bad movie. Jobs cringed from the stink of the man's breath.

"J'ou expecting that big ship to come back for j'ou, eh?" Newton taunted. "Come right down and save j'ou all, kill all us Marauders? J'ou think about taking Marauders with j'ou on that nice big ship?"

Jobs felt as if he was going to faint. The ship? Why was Newton talking about the ship?

"What are you talking about?" Jobs cried. "I'm not . . ."

Newton leaned closer over Jobs, blocking his view of anything but the man's chest.

"Well, I say it not going to happen, that ship come and rescue j'ou. J'ou all stuck here with Marauders. J'ou nothing special. J'ou dirt like all Marauders."

"I never said I was special," Jobs said weakly. "I . . . I'm sorry."

"What's going on here?" It was Mo'Steel.

Newton backed away a few steps and grunted. "He —"

"Jobs first," Mo'Steel snapped.

"I spilled some water," he said, throat ragingly dry now with both thirst and terror. "It was an accident."

Mo'Steel. His best friend. But the leader of the Marauders, too . . .

Mo'Steel looked at Newton. His face was grim.

"How much water? Was it yours?"

"All water belongs to Marauders," Newton said angrily.

"Yeah, and we're Marauders right now, all of us," Mo'Steel replied calmly.

"It was my share," Jobs said. "He still has his. It doesn't affect him!"

Mo'Steel looked steadily at Jobs. It unnerved him.

"Well, Duck, it does affect him," Mo'Steel said. "It affects us all. The team is only as strong as its weakest player and all that. One of us falls down, we all feel it."

Jobs was stunned but not surprised. He knew it, he knew it! Everyone was against him, even his so-called best friend was betraying him. Only Billy. Billy was the only one Jobs could count on. Where was Billy?!

Mo'Steel looked at Newton, who, Jobs saw with fear, was frowning.

"J'ou understand," he said.

"Yeah, I do," Mo'Steel said. "I also understand that it was an accident. Stuff happens, nothing you can do about it but go on. You got your share of water, right? So we're going to let this go and we're all going to be more careful, right, 'migo?"

Newton glared at Jobs but said nothing. Then he nodded at Mo'Steel and stalked off.

Jobs, clutching his empty Beast bladder, slipped past Mo'Steel. He refused to meet his former best friend's eyes.

"Jobs!" Mo'Steel called but Jobs kept on going.

Mo'Steel had gone back to help Jobs when Cocker told him what had happened. Cocker wasn't a bad guy. He said he thought maybe Jobs was sick.

Mo'Steel watched Jobs scurrying away like a frightened mouse. Something was up with his best friend. Something not good. He figured something in the air — something about this place — was driving Jobs mad.

One thing Mo'Steel knew he could not afford — losing Jobs.

Jobs was the reliable one. He was the sensible one, the intelligent one. Since when did Jobs react to a bully like Newton by cringing? Since when did Jobs avoid his own best friend and ally?

Mo'Steel sighed and ran to catch up with the others. No doubt about it. Jobs was soul-sick. Planet Earth was trying to take him.

Question now is, Mo'Steel thought, *how do I stop planet Earth from winning?*

2Face hadn't expected a clear, precise demarcation between the Shadow Zone and the Dark Zone. She'd figured one zone would sort of fade into the other. But when 2Face felt a ripple of tension run through the Marauders, she knew they had officially passed into what the Marauders considered the Dark Zone.

Badger confirmed this.

"Yeah," he said, eyes darting, "this is it. It get colder and darker as j'ou go. But it's bad enough now."

2Face shivered and didn't know if she was really cold or just supposed to be.

It doesn't seem so bad, she told herself, and scoffed at the superstitions that had made the Dark Zone the home of evil creatures like the Beasts. *Just a fairy tale,* she decided. *Just some goofy, spooky story.*

2Face shivered again and stepped up her pace.

CHAPTER SIXTEEN

"YOU WANT TO FIGHT, WE'LL FIGHT TOMORROW."

They'd stopped to rest and eat. And to build a fire.

The Dark Zone. Mo'Steel had flown across part of it, back before the psychotropic storm that had led his group underground.

Now he was actually on the ground of the place. And it was cold.

Mo'Steel settled down between D-Caf and Roger Dodger to eat another gross meal.

"When are we going to get there?" D-Caf muttered. "To where the Beasts are?"

Mo'Steel swatted D-Caf's arm. "What's your rush? Can't wait to see me dead?"

D-Caf's mouth hung open in shock. "No, that's not what I meant."

Mo'Steel sighed. "I know, kid, I know. Now, quiet. Newton looks like he's got something to say."

Newton nodded to the huddled group.

"This here's the Dark Zone," he said loudly. "Some of j'ou don't know much about it. Some of us, we know all about it. There's a lot more than Beasts j'ou have to watch for."

"Then why don't you tell us what we need to know," Mo'Steel replied impatiently. He was beyond tired of the Marauders withholding vital information until the last minute.

Newton grinned maliciously. "J'ou ready for it?"

"Always be prepared," Mo'Steel said. "If we know what to expect, we can better protect ourselves." He eyed Newton steadily before adding: "I can better protect you."

Newton half rose from his seat, his face a mask of fury. But something stopped him, made him sit back down, though still glaring at Mo'Steel.

"J'ou better watch for Slizzers," Newton said, hissing the final word for effect.

"What are Slizzers?" Mo'Steel asked without expression.

"Slizzers are very bad," Newton said. "They love the dark. Slizzers stay close to the ground. J'ou don't see 'em coming, then many, many are suddenly all over j'ou, eating, eating. That's all Slizzers do — eat. Then it's over for j'ou. All that's left of j'ou is bones."

"Why can't you just kill them?" 2Face burst out. "Just decimate the population."

"No, Slizzers can never be done with," Cocker said, shooting Newton a glance that asked for permission to speak. Mo'Steel saw Newton nod and Cocker went on. "The females, they bring on big litters all the time. Slizzers eat and make more Slizzers, that's all they do. And they spit poison. It burn right through j'ou and then they eat j'ou."

"They sound like roaches," Jobs whispered behind Mo'Steel. "Roaches can spit. They like the dark, they eat anything, they reproduce constantly. I wonder —"

"Where did these Slizzers come from?" Mo'Steel asked, cutting off his friend's panicky voice.

Newton nodded now at Sanchez.

"There is a story about the Slizzers," he said, pitching his voice low enough so that Mo'Steel had to lean forward to hear every word. "An old story that comes down through generations, from the end of Before and the beginning of Now. Just like some humans survived what j'ou call the Rock, other creatures did, too. They were the first Slizzers, though they were much smaller and not so bold as what they have become. They lived in nests built in the ruins of Before and ate everything that didn't kill them. Slizzers could eat much that humans couldn't, so while Alphas and Marauders and Savagers struggled, Slizzers grew. They grew big and many until they were so big and so many, they began to prey on humans. Slizzers started killing humans. That's when the Alphas said they were no longer coming up to the surface and since that day, not one of them has. But Marauders?" Sanchez looked around at his band proudly. "We were not sent into hiding. We stayed and struggled and survived."

"Slizzers shed," Badger whispered from behind Mo'Steel and Jobs. "Their skin is like armor. If j'ou lucky and find some, j'ou make protection. Newton, he wears a big piece of Slizzer skin under his shirt. Very hard for anything to get through it. Newton says he snuck up on sleeping Slizzer and cut it up, took its skin. But I say that's a lie."

"Thanks for the tip," Mo'Steel whispered back.

"See?" Jobs whispered excitedly. "Roaches! They shed their exoskeleton. I bet the Slizzers are mutant roaches! Why not? There were about five thousand species of roaches back before."

"Where's the Raid when you need it?" D-Caf quipped. Roger Dodger laughed and Sanchez's expression grew dark.

"So, how do you protect against a raid — uh, I mean, an attack?" Mo'Steel asked.

"J'ou must keep the fire alive all the time in the Dark Zone," Newton said. "Fire and torches must never go out. That's when the Slizzers will attack. Slizzers are very fast on their many legs."

"Maybe that's what I've been hearing all along!" Mo'Steel could hear the growing panic in Jobs's voice. "Slizzers. Their feet scurrying along, watching me, sizing me up. . . ."

Mo'Steel put his hand on Jobs's arm, hoping to calm him, but Jobs pulled away.

"We'll keep the fire strong," he said to Newton. "Whoever takes guard duty tonight has to pay serious attention to the fire, understand? Who's up?"

Balder grinned and nudged Claw.

"Nesia be on guard," he said. "Her and 2Face."

Mo'Steel sighed. Nesia was worthless. But 2Face was tough and could be relied upon. At least when it came down to saving her own butt.

"Okay," he said. "Let's try to get some sleep."

2Face didn't know whether to laugh or to cry when she and Nesia were appointed guards on the same shift. Everyone knew Nesia despised her. Whoever had set this up was definitely looking for trouble.

2Face sighed. She was in no mood for a fight with anyone, human or Slizzer.

Around 2Face the group settled. And Nesia stood just over her, glaring down.

"Why don't you just leave me alone, okay?" 2Face spat out before the idiot could open her mouth.

Nesia stood her ground but said nothing. In the glare of the firelight 2Face thought she looked more than ever like a cartoonish cretin.

Wait, 2Face thought. *Weren't bullies essentially stupid? Weren't they supposed to lose interest if you didn't take their bait? It was worth a try.*

"Look," 2Face said, more pleasantly now, "I'm tired, okay? Let's just watch the stupid fire until our shift is over. You want to fight, we'll fight tomorrow. I'm sure you're tired, too."

Nesia seemed confused by 2Face's words. Confused enough that after a moment she backed off and dropped to the ground on the other side of the fire.

Now if she'd only stop staring at me, 2Face thought. She drew her knees to her chest and rested her forehead on them. *I won't go to sleep,* she vowed. *I'll just rest and I . . .*

Though the fire wasn't huge, 2Face felt its corforting warmth creep into her. The freakin' Dark Zone, even here at the edge, was so freakin' cold.

The fire was nice. It was nice and warm.

And then her mother was screaming and screaming and her father was crying and she was in the midst of it all, half aware of the look of horror on the paramedic's face, half gone far, far away. . . .

"Noooo!"

2Face screamed and came fully aware and yanked her hand from the fire and couldn't stop screaming and watching in horrid fascination as her poor, poor skin bubbled and shriveled. . . .

2Face whimpered and held her burnt hand to her chest. "No more, no more, no more," she wailed.

Suddenly, Olga was kneeling by her side and trying to soothe her. "Let me see your hand; it's okay, let me see it."

2Face let Olga tug lightly on her wrist to bring her burnt hand forward. She was only partially aware of the rumbling of voices around her. It was all very confusing and the pain was sharp and alive.

"It's not bad," Olga crooned, and 2Face sobbed again. "It will be fine, okay? All right?"

And then, a shout. One of the Marauder men. And a woman, crying out.

"Tackie! She's gone! Slizzers got her!"

"Cocker!" someone cried. "Build up the fire. We need torches, too. We're going after them."

Was that Mo'Steel?

"Romeo!" Olga cried. "Be careful!"

2Face felt her head go all fuzzy and heard nothing more for a while.

CHAPTER SEVENTEEN

"I SAY THAT MO'STEEL GOT TO GO."

Violet joined up with the search-and-rescue team. There wasn't any doubt about her going. For all her fear of revealing her mutation to the Marauders, when it came down to the possibility of saving a two-year-old's life, Violet was ready to act.

Assuming, of course, her power to bring a dead person back to life worked on Marauders. Assuming also that if Tackie was already dead, they got to her quickly enough.

The team was comprised of Newton, Balder, Mo'Steel, Eel, and Sanchez. Mo'Steel had given her a look that told her he knew why she'd come along. For that, she was grateful.

In the flare of torchlight, the faces of the Marauder men were more grotesque than they appeared in the flat gray light of the Shadow Zone.

"A trail!" Newton called in a harsh whisper. He angled his torch to reveal a series of deep scratches on the silvery-black surface of Earth's Dark Zone. The scratch marks were intermittent but led on ahead, slightly to the left.

Violet followed. She was cold and she was scared. What if the Slizzers weren't frightened by the glare of their torches? What if she had to go worm and Mo'Steel wasn't able to prevent one of the Marauder men from freaking out and killing her?

"There!"

Sanchez darted ahead and lowered his torch so that it was close to the ground and growled a menacing growl. So quickly she wasn't even sure she was seeing what she saw, Violet caught sight of something long and low and shiny dark in the light of Sanchez's torch. And legs, two legs, something long and slender, something that made a sound like —

A Slizzer! Violet gasped and took a step back into Eel.

Sanchez chased the Slizzer away and then he and Newton and the others began a search of the ground. Violet stuck close to them, hoping they would find Tackie alive, determined that if she were recently dead, she'd go worm to save her, even if it meant her own brutal death.

And then: "Those fools!"

Newton knelt and the others hurried to his side.

"God help us," Mo'Steel murmured.

Violet took one look at what was left of the child and her stomach heaved. There was no way in Heaven or on Earth she could bring Tackie back to life. Her mutation was still a safe secret. Somehow, that fact didn't comfort.

Silently, the group turned and walked back to the band waiting by the now-flaming fire. Violet walked at Mo'Steel's side. She felt bad about leaving Tackie's body alone. But she didn't protest aloud. Tackie had been a Marauder child. It was up to her people to do with her what they would.

When they were only yards away from the rest of the band, Violet heard Aga shout their approach. Coming closer she saw Curia standing alone, face and body tense with hope.

One look at the faces of the returning search party was enough to tell her that her daughter was gone. Curia let out a wail that made Violet slap her hands to her ears.

Aga tried to make Curia drink some water but she pushed the bladder away and flung herself to the ground.

Violet just stood and watched.

*   *   *

The entire band was awake and gathered close to the roaring fire. Mo'Steel had ordered lit torches to be set up in a wider circle around them, as the first line of defense.

"They will be beaten," Newton said harshly, suddenly. "They will learn to consider the good of all Marauders."

"I didn't do anything!" 2Face cried, cradling her bandaged hand in the other. Mo'Steel thought she sounded genuinely scared, chastened. "I'm sorry I fell asleep. I'm sorry the kid got killed. But Nesia attacked me, she's always wanted to get me!"

"It's true," Olga murmured. "I've seen Nesia poke 2Face and trip her and taunt her."

Mo'Steel nodded to acknowledge his mother's information.

Nesia pretended to lunge for 2Face. Aga and Cocker restrained her and Nesia cackled loudly. "Ugly girl afraid of Nesia," she cried.

2Face whimpered and darted closer to Olga and the others. Mo'Steel heard derisive laughter from a male Marauder.

"They'll both be punished," Mo'Steel said loudly. To his own surprise, the crowd quieted and listened.

"And I'll decide the punishment," he added. "Anyone got a problem with that?"

I so seriously hope nobody does, he thought.

There was some grumbling and then, silence.

"J'ou will give punishment," Sanchez said finally.

Mo'Steel took a deep breath.

"Good. This is the way it's going to be. No beatings. Nesia and 2Face, you'll apologize to Curia and then to each and every member of this band. And then you'll divide and shoulder Curia's packs until we get where we're going. Understood?"

2Face looked intensely relieved. "Understood," she said.

Nesia was plainly and wickedly gleeful. She sneered at 2Face. For a brief moment Mo'Steel wondered if he should reverse his decision.

"I'll stand guard now," he said firmly. "Cocker, Badger, you're with me. The rest of you, try to get some sleep."

Newton met with Claw, Snipe, and Balder, men he knew he still could trust, as far as any man could trust another. Which wasn't much.

But Newton wanted to hear what the men thought about who was still on his side.

"Badger." Snipe grunted. "He one who think that Mo'Steel a good leader. I say that Mo'Steel got to go."

Newton was not surprised but still glad to hear Snipe's opinion.

"Who else j'ou think we got?" Newton asked.

Claw held up his seven stubby fingers and began to count off.

"Nesia. Grost, she go with j'ou. Curia, yeah. She blame the ugly girl for the Slizzers getting Tackie."

"Who else?" Newton pressed.

Balder laughed. "J'ou got Balder and Snipe and Claw. Who else you need?"

Newton backhanded Balder across his scruffy face. "Shut up."

Claw went on. "J'ou got Rattler."

Newton snorted. "When he not drunk. What about Eel? And Sanchez?"

Snipe said, "J'ou got Aga. Maybe. Eel, don't know, maybe yes. Sanchez, I seen him look at pretty blond girl. He like way she tell a story. But Sanchez never break with Marauder tradition."

Newton listened and thought. Yorka didn't count, and neither did the young ones. Still, if he could get Eel behind him solid, he'd be in. Badger and Aga were of no real account. A kid and a woman, easy to force on to his side. Or to eliminate.

Newton considered the dramatic value of Mo'Steel's being brutally torn apart and eaten alive by the ferocious Beasts, in full view of his worthless friends. In full view of the Marauders.

Newton grinned. Yeah, he'd let the Beasts take care of Mo'Steel. And when they'd done with him Newton would claim leadership. And if anyone had any trouble with that, well, he'd just stick them in the gut with a knife and some of that poison he'd taken off Hawk.

Yeah, Newton would be the new Marauder leader when Mo'Steel lost the battle.

If Mo'Steel lost the battle.

Newton shifted uncomfortably. *Now, where had those words come from?* he wondered.

He shook himself and squinted over to where Mo'Steel stood guard with Cocker and Badger. At a distance, the kid didn't look like much. *Doesn't look like much up close, either,* Newton reminded himself sternly.

"J'ou got a plan?" Claw said, digging in his nose with the longest of his stubby fingers.

Newton grunted. He'd say nothing more for the time being.

CHAPTER EIGHTEEN

"STAY AWAY, GHOSTS."

Mo'Steel was tired. *The leg could use some rest,* he thought. But maybe they should go on for a while. Maybe . . .

Badger appeared at Mo'Steel's side.

"J'ou need to stop now," he said softly, "for the leg."

"What are you, a mind reader?" Mo'Steel quipped.

Badger shrugged. "I see things. It's okay to stop now. No one will complain."

Jeez, I've got me a sidekick, Mo'Steel thought.

Mo'Steel nodded. "Cool."

He raised a hand and called out, "We rest here."

The band stopped. No one objected. Badger grinned.

Quickly but efficiently, a temporary camp was laid out. Meager portions of food were passed around.

Mo'Steel noted, not for the first time, that the men's portions were larger than the women's. The children got a portion somewhere between the two.

Mo'Steel had been slipping some of his own rations into his mother's. He doubted she was aware of his actions — the headache interfered with her tracking the small things — and was glad. She'd only try to give the food back.

After the band had eaten, Newton withdrew a tiny, ancient glass bottle, clearly a relic from pre-Rock days, from the inner breast pocket of his tunic. In the flickering firelight, Mo'Steel thought he saw a thick, milky liquid inside.

Newton took a sip, eyeing Mo'Steel with what looked like a challenge, then passed the bottle to his left.

"J'ou should be the first to drink," Badger said under his breath. "J'ou the leader. Newton knows this."

"He dissed me, man," Mo'Steel said with a feeble attempt at levity. "What is it, anyway?"

"They say it's taken from inside young Beasts," Badger said, making a face. "Hawk and Newton stole it from the Savagers. All I know is it makes your head all loose."

"I stay away from it," Badger said, "too dangerous. Some like it better, like Rattler. And Nesia."

Badger moved off to sit with Sanchez. Mo'Steel saw both refuse the bottle when it came around.

By the time the bottle came to Mo'Steel, Newton and those others who had been first to drink were working on another tiny bottle.

Mo'Steel sniffed the grubby bottle of thick, viscous stuff warily. "Oh, man, that's foul!"

"What did you expect?" Violet said.

"Not much. It doesn't matter. I'm not drinking it."

"Are we going to offend them if we don't?" D-Caf asked nervously.

"Probably," Violet said. "But I wouldn't worry about it. Look around. Pretty much everyone's out cold."

Mo'Steel looked. Violet was right. The kids were all asleep. Badger and Sanchez were talking quietly, their backs to the group. The women who weren't snoring were busy putting away packets of food and tending to the fire. Most of the men lay flat on their backs, unmoving.

Mo'Steel crawled a few feet away from the group and emptied what remained of the gross liquid into the ash. Then he crawled back and tossed the bottle into the center of the rough ring.

"That stuff must be brutal," Mo'Steel said. "A half an hour and they're annihilated."

"Too annihilated for trouble, maybe," Olga said. "Maybe we can all get some real sleep. Only worry about the Beasts. And the Slizzers."

Mo'Steel laughed softly. "Sounds good to me, Mom," he said. "Wake me when it's supposed to be morning."

Claw and Rattler were on guard. Jobs thought the choice of Rattler as guard was lame; the guy was seriously drunk, muttering and gesticulating wildly. Claw wasn't in much better shape; his large head was bobbing toward his chest. Still, Jobs was so tired and cold he was grateful he himself wasn't on guard duty.

Jobs took one last look around the group before settling down. The Marauders and the *Mayflower* survivors were hunkered down in the ash, dirty, voluminous clothes wrapped around them for warmth, a rough collection of lumps, like an outcrop of rocks, still in the blackness.

"Stay away, ghosts," Jobs mumbled, and closed his eyes.

CHAPTER NINETEEN

"J'OU DON'T DO ANYTHING FOOLISH."

Jobs woke to a scream that was so close and so frightened, it seemed to be coming from his own mouth.

Madly, he tore away the skins covering him while urging his eyes to adjust to the surrounding gloom, lit erratically by the dying fire.

Dying fire? Jobs's brain came into full awake mode with the recognition of the fact that the fire should not be dying. Not if the guards had been doing their job.

All around was chaos. Everyone was on his or her feet. Everyone but Jobs.

The scream. It had been a woman's and now was replaced by terrible, sad sobbing.

"It's Olga!"

Jobs stumbled to his feet as Violet rushed past

him. Jobs whirled, located his best friend's mother. She was gasping, reaching for words.

"He put his hand over my mouth. . . ."

Jobs saw Mo'Steel fly past him. Jobs reached out and grabbed his friend's arm, aware that Badger had grabbed his friend's other arm and that they were restraining him with difficulty.

"J'ou don't do anything foolish," Badger hissed.

Mo'Steel thrashed wildly, eyes blazing.

"Mo, no!" Jobs cried, but it was no use. Mo'Steel slipped from his hold and tossed off Badger's grip as easily. Jobs had never seen his friend look so crazed, almost possessed.

Rattler crawled to his feet, laughing, muttering. Jobs wasn't sure Rattler even knew what he'd just tried to do.

Mo'Steel strode over to the drunken Marauder. No one else tried to stop him.

And before Jobs's brain could process what his eyes were seeing, Mo'Steel's right arm stuck out straight before him and Rattler seemed to lean into Mo'Steel's face and Mo'Steel stepped back and his arm came with him and Rattler crumpled at his feet.

Then Jobs saw the blood slowly seeping from under the crumpled layers of clothing and felt dizzy.

"J'ou hurt him." That was Badger, crouching now beside Rattler's body. "J'ou get him right in the gut."

Before Jobs could speak his horror, the women, most wielding a torch, swarmed Rattler's crumpled body and began to strip it of clothing, tools, and weapons. It was like watching vultures pick and tear apart the body of a cow, the process both disgusting and impressive in its efficiency.

Mo'Steel stood panting and watched the women swarm over Rattler's body. Newton and the other men were staring at him. Mo'Steel felt their eyes on him, felt the mingled emotions emanating from their bodies — hate, grudging respect, a small amount of fear — but refused to meet any man's gaze. Instead, he focused on the crouching women.

Aga, Curia, and Yorka came to Mo'Steel now, laden with Rattler's belongings. Mo'Steel saw a new look of respect in their eyes.

"This is for j'ou, leader Mo'Steel," Aga said, holding out Rattler's weapon, a long knife.

Mo'Steel took the weapon reluctantly. But he couldn't bring himself to accept the dead man's clothes.

"Give the cleanest, best clothing to the kids," he directed, hearing his own voice as from a great distance. "I want nothing but the weapon for myself. Whatever's left over, let the women distribute evenly among themselves."

This act of generosity seemed to further impress the Marauder women. Nesia leered at him in what she probably thought was a seductive way. Even Grost seemed to register Mo'Steel's act as something extraordinary. She smiled briefly, then covered her face with her hands.

"Say something," a voice at Mo'Steel's ear hissed. It was 2Face. "Say something to the men."

Mo'Steel looked down at 2Face and in the dancing firelight thought she looked like a biblical demon.

"They got the message," he mumbled.

Then it was his mother before him, face tear-streaked, eyes darker than ever with sorrow.

Olga took his hand in both of hers — the hand that had held the murder weapon — and kissed it.

"I'm sorry, Romeo," she whispered. "I'm so sorry."

Mo'Steel felt the tears begin to flood his eyes. He didn't bother to wipe them away.

CHAPTER TWENTY

IT WAS TIME.

Newton sat up abruptly. He squinted into the darkness. His nostrils quivered, his fingers tingled with certainty.

Yeah, the Beasts, they were close. They were close and they were watching.

Newton might not have killed any Beasts, like he claimed, but he knew when they were near. He hadn't expected them yet; he'd thought maybe the band would have to travel farther into the Dark Zone before the Beasts made themselves known.

But here they were. Maybe the smell of blood had drawn them. Rattler's blood. For a moment back then Newton had thought the kid Mo'Steel would kill him next. But he hadn't.

Newton scrambled to his feet and was assaulted by memory.

It was a long, long time ago, when Newton was

just a kid. He and Hawk had been attacked by three massive Beasts. Hawk had managed to wound all three. Newton had kept back, scared, shouting useless insults at the Beasts. Finally, Hawk had emerged from the dark, wounded but alive.

Newton had never forgotten the look of loathing on his brother's face when it emerged in the torchlight. Loathing for the Beasts? Or loathing for his spineless brother?

Newton shook off the unsettling memory and roused the band.

It was time.

Soon he would be the leader.

Mo'Steel had been asleep, as deeply asleep as he'd ever been since this stupid journey had begun.

"Nice timing, Beasts," he muttered, getting to his feet. He began to stretch and flex, allowed the adrenaline to flow back — the adrenaline that had so recently helped him to kill Rattler.

Kill to kill again. Was that the phrase? he wondered. *Or was it, Live to kill again?*

"J'ou want to know what will happen?" Badger said, appearing out of the torchlit dark.

"Uh, yeah," Mo'Steel said with a forced smile. "Sure, lay it on me."

But Newton's big, bragging voice interrupted, calling everyone to listen.

"The Beasts, they be here now, watching. Waiting. J'ou," he cried, pointing to Mo'Steel. "J'ou got to go out to those Beasts." Now Newton pointed to himself. "I will stay here and protect the others."

Mo'Steel didn't answer. What was there to say at this point? He was tired and he'd killed two men and he knew he'd kill again if it got him some decent food and some aspirin for his mother. He'd just strap it up now and go off and try his damndest to kill him a Beast.

"Remember," Badger said, as if reading his thoughts, "j'ou got to get the head Beast. The leader."

"How will I know him?" Mo'Steel asked, tying back his unruly hair with a piece of string.

"He the biggest one, most times."

Very precise definition, Mo'Steel thought.

"How will I stop them from swarming the others back here?" he asked, securing Rattler's long knife in his belt.

Olga had joined them now, and Aga, and Noyze.

"Remember what Newton said," Aga told him. "If j'ou separate the leader, the others, they will back away. We will be okay until j'ou kill the leader."

"And if I don't kill the leader?" Mo'Steel asked. Aga's eyes were sad.

"Then the Beasts will swarm. Many will be dead."

Noyze took his arm and laid her head on his shoulder.

"Romeo . . ." Olga began.

"Yeah, Mom, I know. Be careful."

"Yes. No. Just — kill him, okay? Just — kill the leader."

Noyze let him go and Mo'Steel hugged his mother close and felt her tears against his neck.

"Stay with Aga," he said, releasing her. "Until I come back."

Mo'Steel was aware that he had an audience. An audience behind him — Marauders, his mom, and the rest — and an audience before him. The Beasts.

He walked on, slowly, eyes squinting into the dark as he left the immediate glare of the firelight, looking for darker shapes, looking for the Beasts.

"Come out, come out, wherever you are," he sang softly.

And then — they did.

Mo'Steel stopped dead. Four, maybe five dark and hulking shapes seemed to rise from the black

ground ahead of him, maybe five, six yards away —
too close for comfort.

Try as he might, Mo'Steel couldn't make out any
one shape that was larger than the others, not at
this distance. His hand was tense around the long
knife, his heart beat painfully in his chest and was
loud in his ears. Hand and heart. Those were the
things he had to rely on now.

Strength and courage.

"Hey," he said, voice quivering with energy, "can
we get this going? Why don't you guys just swarm
and get it over with?"

Mo'Steel jumped back, then crouched, long knife
ready, because as if they'd understood his challenge,
the four — no, five — dark shapes surged forward,
squealing to make Mo'Steel want to cover his ears.

*Get the leader, get the leader, cut him out of the
herd.* The words chanted in Mo'Steel's head as he
sprang out of the way of the fastest of the Beasts,
and whirled to avoid another, smaller one.

As he dodged and darted, Mo'Steel's brain registered the fact that, yeah, these Beasts were mutant
rats, big honkin' ones.

And then, running, looking over his shoulder,
Mo'Steel saw him. The leader, no doubt about it. The

guy was at least half again the size of the next biggest Beast.

I ain't no cowboy, Mo'Steel thought, *but I'd give anything for a horse and a lasso right now.*

With a whoop of crazed but deliberate energy, Mo'Steel reversed direction and with the long knife held out straight before him, he ran straight at the leader, glaring directly into the Beast's big shining eyes.

Vaguely, in the seconds it took Mo'Steel to get within fighting distance of the Beast leader, he was aware of the other Beasts falling back. When he skidded to a stop, he knew that the other Beasts were out of sight but still watching.

He'd managed to isolate the leader. *How about that,* Mo'Steel thought, *I did it.*

But the thought gave him no real satisfaction. Face-to-face with the massive leader, Mo'Steel saw clearly that the Beast was not in the least bit afraid.

And no doubt about it: There was a gleam of intelligence in those beady eyes, a gleam of purpose — *kill this human enemy. This is our territory,* the eyes said, *and you are not welcome.*

With a leap so fast Mo'Steel had no time to evade it, the Beast crashed down on him, slamming him flat on his back. Mo'Steel felt his brain slosh against the inside of his skull and his eyes roll up into his head.

It was a moment before he could see straight again and when he could, all he saw was — fur. Stinking, dark fur.

Mo'Steel gagged. The stench of the Beast's fur was overwhelming, different from the stench of the average Marauder, more wild and alive. The Beast straddled him, its four massive, wrinkled legs on either side of Mo'Steel's quivering body, its long, pointy nose less than an inch from Mo'Steel's grimacing face. The Beast's sharp yellow teeth were bared and dripped saliva onto Mo'Steel's exposed neck. He cursed under his breath as the saliva stung and burned into his skin.

More scars, he thought inanely, then: *Scars only matter to the living. Don't jump to conclusions.*

As if he'd read his victim's thoughts, the Beast reared onto its hind legs and uttered a shriek of triumph. It was all Mo'Steel needed. With every shred of agility he had left, Mo'Steel yanked his legs up toward his chest and in one clean motion, kicked up at the Beast, hitting it under the ribs, stunning it enough to send it backing up just enough for Mo'Steel to slip back and away. Mo'Steel crouched, long knife ready, and taunted the now-furious Beast.

"You want me, you stinking furball, well, come get me!" he shouted.

Eyes snapping with rage, the Beast lunged forward and Mo'Steel lunged forward as well, keeping low, and the Beast dropped down onto him — and the knife.

As the Beast dropped, Mo'Steel rolled out from under it, reeking, hot blood coating his head and shoulders and arm, his damaged thigh screeching, his heart beating double-time, adrenaline making him leap to his feet to catch his enemy's next move.

But there was no next move.

Mo'Steel stood panting, ready, long knife held aloft, but the Beast didn't come after him. The Beast lay on the dark and ashy ground, black blood pooling from under its wet, matted fur.

And its eyes. Mo'Steel was mesmerized by the Beast's dead and staring eyes. Even in death, the eyes of the massive Beast were furious with disbelief.

"Sorry, big guy," Mo'Steel mumbled, and wiped his brow with the back of his hand. "Had to be done."

"He is the true leader!"

Vaguely, Mo'Steel became aware that people were shouting, that someone was laughing gleefully, that someone . . .

Was sneaking up in the dark behind him!

"Romeo! Look out!"

Mo'Steel crouched, whirled, held the long knife at the ready. . . .

With a shriek of fury Newton came charging at him . . .

CHAPTER TWENTY-ONE

"SHE'S PRETTY COOL."

Jobs automatically, unthinkingly, rushed forward but strong hands grabbed him and held him back. Claw on one side, Snipe on the other, laughing cruelly.

"Newton's cheating!" Roger Dodger cried. "He's cheating!"

"Someone stop them!" Noyze screamed.

All crazy thoughts of Mo'Steel's imagined betrayal left Jobs's head in a rush. His head was clear: Mo'Steel had to live.

Suddenly — Jobs felt a surge of triumph mixed inextricably with a lance of fear. That slight glimmer . . . It was Edward, it had to be! Edward, all but invisible, close to the wrestling men and — yes! Something small and gleaming shot down, then shot back up. Whatever it was had punctured the back of Newton's right thigh.

Newton roared and must have loosened his death grip on Mo'Steel because suddenly, Mo'Steel was standing over Newton, the tip of his long knife at the big man's throat. Jobs saw Mo'Steel kick something out of reach and imagined it was Newton's weapon. Claw and Snipe let go of Jobs in their surprise and in the dark around him Jobs could hear the excitement and mingled reactions of the Marauders and his fellow Remnants.

"Oh, yes, oh, please," Olga murmured close to Jobs.

Aga stood next to Olga and Jobs saw her link arms with Mo'Steel's mother, her face intense as she watched the final stage of the unexpected battle.

Jobs inched closer to Mo'Steel and Newton. Balder, Claw, and Snipe stood now with weapons drawn, but unmoving. They seemed fascinated by the sight of their ringleader flat on his back, at the mercy of a kid.

And then:

"Savagers!"

Cocker sounded the cry, and Jobs saw him point into the far distance.

"Where? I don't see anything!" Jobs cried.

"Savagers are coming," Cocker repeated grimly, assuredly.

"Cocker knows," Badger said, coming up beside Jobs, a vague Edward in tow. "Trust him."

Jobs stared hard at where Edward should be.

"Where did you get the knife?" he said.

"Grost," Edward said simply. "She's pretty cool."

Savagers coming. *Okay*, Mo'Steel thought. That bit of information meant he'd have to hurry things along.

Mo'Steel held the point of Rattler's long knife at Newton's throat. A thin trickle of blood tried to run down Newton's neck but got clogged in thickets of dirt and sweat.

"I could kill you," Mo'Steel said, his voice oddly calm in spite of the heaving of his chest. "I should kill you. You've been after me and my people since the start. I know you put Nesia up to shoving 2Face into the fire. I know you told Balder to force those drugs on D-Caf. I know you put the idea of attacking my mother in Rattler's head. And I'm betting the tip of your knife is dipped in poison."

"No," Newton whimpered.

"Don't lie to me," Mo'Steel roared. Then, in a more normal voice, he added, "It wouldn't be smart."

Mo'Steel noticed for the first time a craven look on the Marauder's face and realized that for all his posturing and bullying, Newton wasn't in the least bit brave. Smart, maybe. Big, yes. But a hero? No.

I am the hero of this tale, Mo'Steel told himself, and with that realization came a surge of magnanimous feeling.

Mo'Steel withdrew the point of the knife slowly and took a step back from Newton's prone form.

"Get up," he commanded.

Newton lay still, eyes wide and unblinking, uncomprehending.

"I said, get up."

"What j'ou do to me?" Newton gasped, and Mo'Steel heard a sudden panicky fear in the man's voice.

"I'm letting you live, you moron. It's called I win and you lose so I can do whatever I want. And what I want is to let your sorry butt live. So, get up. Before I change my mind."

Newton crawled to his feet and immediately swayed. Mo'Steel stuck out his arm and balanced the man.

"Let Aga get you fixed up," he said neutrally. "I'm going to need you to fight again soon. Oh, yeah. And I'm gonna need that poison you took off Hawk."

"How did j'ou —"

Mo'Steel cut Newton off. "It's a leader's job to know things. Now, go with Aga."

Aga came forward. Mo'Steel picked up Newton's poisoned blade and gave it to the woman.

"Use it if you have to," he told her.

Aga peered warily at Newton before taking his arm and leading him aside.

"Mo'Steel!"

Mo'Steel turned toward Noyze.

"Do you see what I see, with the Savagers? Look!"

Mo'Steel squinted through the dark. No doubt. Unmistakable, the two hideous heads and the hoverboards.

"Oh, yeah." Mo'Steel almost laughed. "Looks like we just found our two remaining Riders. Figures they'd side with the enemy."

Nesia cried out. "Them Savagers, they's got some more Beasts! We going to die!"

A ripple of wonder and fear ran through the Marauders at the sight of the Riders. Grost covered her eyes. Curia yelped. Prota gripped Croce's arm and even the macho little boy looked scared.

"Calm down," Mo'Steel ordered.

2Face grinned. "Listen to him," she said. "Those

things aren't Beasts. They're just aliens. You know, from outer space. Evil aliens, come to eat you up and spit out your bones."

"Shut up, 2Face," Mo'Steel commanded. "Nesia, get a grip. Yorka, you take the little kids and stand behind. Everyone else, get armed. Jobs?"

Jobs stepped up to Mo'Steel. Mo'Steel looked at him inquisitively.

"You okay, Duck?" he said quietly.

Jobs nodded. "Yeah. I'm okay. And boy, am I glad you won."

Mo'Steel grinned and turned back to the group.

"The Marauders are going to fight and we're going to win." He looked to Newton, who stood with Aga, bent double, panting. "Am I right, Newton?" he said, finding that his voice held a new tone of authority and self-assurance.

"J'ou's right," Newton replied, standing taller, though clearly it was an effort.

Mo'Steel looked at each of the fighting group in turn, met everyone's eyes, and gathered them in this way.

"Okay," he said then, just as a fierce, wild Savager cry came hurtling through the air. "Time to kick some bad-guy butt."

K.A. APPLEGATE

REMNANTS™

(13)

Survival

"WHY WAS SHE STILL ALIVE?"

Yago was coming.

Tate watched him approach slowly, her eyes narrowed down to slits. A tiny dot on the horizon, but definitely Yago. She could make out the white shirt, green hair. She recognized his stride.

He was alone. That was interesting.

Tate dozed. When she woke, Yago was closer. She could see he didn't look too good. His head was too small — no, his neck was too big. Also interesting. A puzzle. She'd always like doing puzzles.

Another long stretch of time passed, Yago continued striding toward her, and now Tate could see the bruises stretching from his collarbone up over his chin. "Couldn't have happened to a nicer guy," Tate said out loud. She was surprised to hear how raspy her own voice sounded. How long had she gone without water? She had no way of counting time. A day. Two?

Tate amused herself watching Yago. She didn't move. Not even when one of his cruddy-looking sneakers touched her knee.

"Come with me," Yago said. He spoke in a half-dead monotone. He was missing a patch of hair over his right ear. As Tate watched, his hand went up automatically. He yanked a few brownish hairs out by their roots and let them drift to the floor. This was not a sign of mental health.

"What happened to your throat?"

"Come on," Yago repeated dully.

"Amelia do that?" Tate could see the flechette gun sticking out of the pocket of Yago's jeans. She wondered why he hadn't drawn it. Maybe he'd forgotten he had it. He looked as if he hadn't slept in a week.

"I said, come on."

"No."

"No?"

"I'm not going anywhere with you," Tate said calmly. "I like it —"

Yago leaned over and grabbed her face. Stared at her.

"*Come. On.*"

Yago grabbed her arm and started pulling her up. He grunted, yanking Tate up onto her knees. Now he was starting to tick her off. If he wanted to kill her, fine. But she wasn't into a forced march.

She tried to give him a shove. The effort sent her stumbling. Her knees buckled. She hadn't stood up in who knew how long. Her legs wouldn't support her. She fell awkwardly onto one knee.

Yago snarled like a rabid dog. He pulled the flechette gun out and swung it at her face.

Tate put up her hands. She halfheartedly tried to reach whatever it was inside her that turned her into the Mouth. From somewhere in her memory came the sound of a link ringing, ringing, ringing . . .

Something connected with her skull. She saw a burst of red light and then nothing.

A secretive *shush-shushing*. Tate's brain played pictures for her, trying to make sense of the sound. . . .

She was in study hall with her heavy chemistry textbook on her knees. Yvonne Flattery and Susan Nichols were whispering in the row behind her —

Shush-shush . . .

She was moving cautiously through a Rider swamp, the wind whistling through the weird bending trees —

Shush-shush . . .

She was on a camping trip with the Camp Fire Girls. She could see herself sleeping peacefully, a fire dancing around the brave circle of tents. The fire spreading slowly through the dry grasses until her nylon tent went up with a soft *woof!* Her sleeping bag was aflame, and her hair —

Her hair was on fire!

Tate's eyes popped open and she found herself lying on her back, watching the glassy ceiling of the basement pass overhead. Yago was dragging her across the basement by her hair. The shushing sounds were her clothes dragging over the floor.

"Stop," she muttered feebly. Then, louder, more urgently — "Stop!"

Yago stopped. He let go of her hair. Tate rolled into a fetal position and lay there feeling miserable.

Why was she still alive? Why didn't Yago just get rid of her? Tate turned her face to the ground and groaned.

Yago nudged her with his shoe. "Come on. Let's go."

"Go where?" Tate mumbled.

"Amelia wants to — see you."

"Oh — so now you're Amelia's errand boy?"

"No!"

Yago's voice. There was something wrong about it. His usual arrogant tone was gone. His lofty messianic tones were gone. He sounded — scared.

Tate opened her eyes and looked up at Yago.

"Come on," Yago repeated.

Tate got to her knees and pulled herself shakily to her feet. She actually wanted to see Amelia now. Yago was pathetic. But maybe Amelia — well, maybe Amelia would help her draw this little drama to an end somehow. Tate didn't have the energy to hope for a happy ending. She was ready to settle for any ending at all.

"Which way?" Tate asked.

"Upstairs," Yago said. His expression was hard to read. Tate thought she saw something like relief mingling with wariness.

She took a step toward the elevator before she realized what Yago was telling her. Her guilt and inadequacy welled up. "Amelia is upstairs? I think — I was looking for her down here. Isn't she controlling the ship from one of the pits?"

Yago shook his head no and gestured toward the elevator with his chin. They walked single file with

Tate in the lead. Yago was silent — no wisecracks, no self-aggrandizing remarks, no lewd comments. Geez, Tate thought, maybe whatever Amelia was doing to him wasn't so bad. . . .

The elevator moved silently upward, and seconds later they were walking out under the towering arches into the alien hallway. Tate stepped forward cautiously — half-expecting Amelia or Charlie to jump out and tackle her. Nothing. The place felt as deserted as the basement.

Tate relaxed for a moment — and then the smell hit her. It was a humid, salty smell. The smell of growing things — like the sea at low tide.

Tate felt a squirt of fear in her belly. Adrenaline pumped into her veins. She looked around wildly, trying to locate the origin of the smell.

Yago stood a few steps behind her, grinning, and then laughing at her. Laughing at her sudden fear. She felt like smacking him. Yelling at him to shut up.

Because she *was* afraid. Somehow, intuitively, she knew this smell was bad. That earthy, organic smell didn't belong on this cold, dead ship.

Then the sounds filtered into her consciousness. She didn't know how she had missed them at first. Moist sounds that went on and on. They sounded — greedy. Like a baby sucking his soggy thumb or a derrick pulling oil from the ground.

"What is that?" Tate whispered.

"Go on to the bridge," Yago said. "See for yourself."

Tate hesitated.

She didn't want to get closer to that smell, that sound. But — she couldn't run away. She knew she would eventually come face-to-face with whatever was on the bridge. She preferred to face it on her feet. Delay would only make her weaker, more afraid.

Tate pushed down her fear. She took a step forward. And then another. She had to go fast or not at all. Yago stayed right behind her, making sure she went through the doorway onto the bridge and then blocking her way out. Tate wasn't sure what she was expecting but it wasn't —

Webs.

The machinery, the computers, the clean architecture of the bridge — it had all been covered by webs.

Something like spider webs.

But no, that wasn't quite right. These were webs but they weren't clean and precisely built like the webs of spiders. No — these were more like dirty cotton candy. Ugly, dirty swatches of grayish fuzz that made Tate long for a big can of Raid. She remembered a sweet old lady from her neighborhood setting fire to the gypsy moth nests that appeared in the trees around their apartment buildings.

You'd need an inferno to take out these webs. They were huge — dirty wrappings stretching from the towering supporting struts all the way down to the chairs just a few feet from where Tate stood.

Tate's gaze darted to three lumpish masses inside the webs. They were writhing, squirming. Vaguely human forms. Amelia. Charlie. Duncan.

So.

This was their evolution.

This was how the Troika had achieved their "advanced form." Tate could almost pity them. They were nothing but bugs. It was almost — sad.

But then — then her eye caught on a fourth lump, smaller than the others and covered in some sort of white goo — and her sadness turned to disgust. She could just make out a familiar jointed shape. It was the leg of a Rider. The leg was about all that was left.

Tate took a fast step back and whacked into Yago. He stood firmly in the doorway, blocking her escape.

"Why — why did you bring me here?" Tate asked, now cold with fear.

"Cells," Yago said bitterly. "As it turns out, living cells are the Troika's favorite snack food. I guess their big transformation is giving them the munchies, and since all of the Meanies and Riders are dead, you're going to be recycled. Sorry, but dem's the breaks."

Tate let a beat pass as she absorbed this bizarre explanation. Had Yago finally slipped into true madness?

No, no — the evidence was here! The Troika wanted to — they wanted to eat her like they'd eaten that Rider. No. Please no —

While Tate's brain skipped, Yago moved swiftly behind her and grabbed her by the wrists. Tate sensed a movement above her — inside the web.

No!

She didn't want to die like a fly caught in a spider web.

How could Yago do this to her? Tate thought wildly. How could he do it to any living being?

He was Evil.

He was Betrayal.

Tate felt barely like herself.

Something was happening. She was seeing in red, everything in red. And brighter than everything else, the Enemy. . . .

Light-Years From Home...And On Their Own

☐	BGA 0-590-87997-9	Remnants	#1: The Mayflower Project	$4.99 US
☐	BGA 0-590-88074-8	Remnants	#2: Destination Unknown	$4.99 US
☐	BGA 0-590-88078-0	Remnants	#3: Them	$4.99 US
☐	BGA 0-590-88193-0	Remnants	#4: Nowhere Land	$4.99 US
☐	BGA 0-590-88194-9	Remnants	#5: Mutation	$4.99 US
☐	BGA 0-590-88195-7	Remnants	#6: Breakdown	$4.99 US
☐	BGA 0-590-88196-5	Remnants	#7: Isolation	$4.99 US
☐	BGA 0-590-88273-2	Remnants	#8: Mother, May I?	$4.99 US
☐	BGA 0-590-88492-1	Remnants	#9: No Place Like Home	$4.99 US
☐	BGA 0-590-88494-8	Remnants	#10: Lost and Found	$4.99 US
☐	BGA 0-590-88495-6	Remnants	#11: Dream Storm	$4.99 US
☐	BGA 0-590-88522-7	Remnants	#12: Aftermath	$4.99 US

Available wherever you buy books, or use this order form.

Scholastic Inc., P.O. Box 7502, Jefferson City, MO 65102

Please send me the books I have checked above. I am enclosing $_____ (please add $2.00 to cover shipping and handling). Send check or money order—no cash or C.O.D.s please.

Name_____Birth date_____

Address_____

City_____State/Zip_____

Please allow four to six weeks for delivery. Offer good in U.S.A. only. Sorry, mail orders are not available to residents of Canada. Prices subject to change.

Continue the exciting journey online at **www.scholastic.com/remnants**

SCHOLASTIC   REMBL503

If it was the end of the world, what would you do?

Check out the official

REMNANTS™

Web site at

http://www.scholastic.com/remnants

and

- Tell the world what you would do if an asteroid was heading toward Earth.

- Play "The Escape" and discover if you have what it takes to secure a berth on the *Mayflower*.

- Find out information about the Remnants, including who is still alive.

Log on...while you still have a chance.

REMT303